LYCAON

WES PARKER

This is a work of fiction. Names, characters, places, and incidents either are the product of the author's imagination or are used fictitiously. Any resemblance to actual persons, living or dead, events, or locales is entirely coincidental

Lycaon

Cover and Art Design by José Lucas, https://twitter.com/Kid_Mindfreak
Map by Niklas Wisedt, www.wistedt.net

ISBN-13: 978-1-7323272-4-5

FOR MOM, WHO ALWAYS TOLD ME TO REACH FOR THE STARS.

MAP OF THE LUNAR SURFACE

PROLOGUE

Dr. Alana Chang wiped the dripping blood from her face. She was doing her best to keep quiet while hiding beneath the lab desk. She didn't understand how it all went so wrong and so fast. Dr. Popov had been such a good man. She didn't know what had happened to him or why he was doing any of this. Just a few days ago, he was one of humanity's most brilliant minds, and now—

A scream erupted from the hallway, followed by a sick guttural laughter that sounded more beast than human. Alana pressed herself up to the back of the desk and held her breath in anticipation. The laboratory doors slid open, and she heard the slow, methodical footsteps of someone entering the room. A little part of her held out hope that it was Lt. Colonel Scott Jackson. That hope was quickly shattered when Dr. Popov began to speak.

"Alana? Come out, come out wherever you are..."

Alana could hear the doctor as he stalked around the laboratory. He tapped his nails on the table as he methodically made his way around.

"Honestly, Alana, you've always been one of my brightest students, so I don't know why you are defying me now? I am sorry about your face. If you would just come out, then we could talk about this. It wasn't my goal to hurt anyone, let alone you. Besides, we all know that I wouldn't have had to resort to this if you hadn't gone and tattled on me." Dr. Popov almost growled the words as he began to lumber around the table.

Alana shot up from her hiding place and sprinted towards the lab doors. She knew it was a futile attempt. Even if she could get away from him, her suit was compromised. Still, she wasn't about to go down without a fight. As she entered the blood-stained hallway, she felt something tight grip her forearm. Pain radiated throughout her entire arm as Dr. Popov's nails dug into her skin. She turned around to look at the man who she used to see as a father figure. Now all she saw was a monster full of hunger.

"You fucking little bitch I'm going to slaughter you like the rabbit that you are Alana. Others have already accepted my gift. Do you think you're better than them? THAN ME?"

Alana tried to pull away, but it was no use. Dr. Popov only dug his nails in deeper, causing her to yell out in pain. Her yell caused a sick smile to grow across his face. The doctor was clearly enjoying himself as he pulled her closer. Dr. Popov stretched his mouth open, showing grotesque amounts of pinkish drool. Alana wasn't sure if the doctor was trying to bite her or kiss her.

A shape appeared out of the corner of her eye, running full speed into Dr. Popov. The sudden impact made the doctor release her, causing her to fall back onto the sticky floor. She pushed herself back to her feet and saw Scott, bloodied and mangled, wrestling with Dr. Popov. Just a few hours ago, Scott would've had no issue overpowering the doctor, but that was no longer the case. Alana stood there, not sure if she should help or make a run for it.

"Run Alana! Get to Armstrong! Hurry!" Jackson yelled through gritted teeth.

"I'm sorry Scott, I'm so sorry." Alana turned and sprinted towards the command center, tears and blood running down her face. Just as she turned the corner to the command center, she heard Scott scream in pain. Alana wanted to go back and help him but knew that she couldn't. For all she knew, he was already dead. She ran to the command center computer and began entering the lockdown commands. Her adrenaline spiked when she heard Dr. Popov yell after her.

"ALANA!" he roared. She could hear him running around the corridor after her. She frantically pressed the keyboard, even though the lockdown had already been initiated. The doors seemed like they were closing slower than usual. She saw Dr. Popov turn the corner of the corridor and decided to make a run for it. If Alana was going to survive this, she needed to find a new EVA suit. She flinched at the sound of Dr. Popov slamming into the blast doors.

"Alana, open this fucking door!" he yelled in an animalistic tone. Alana was pretty sure that the door could contain Dr. Popov, but she wasn't about to stay here and find out. She knew that right now, the smartest thing she could do was listen to Scott. Alana's only chance of survival was if she made it to Armstrong Base. Dr. Popov continued to beat on the door as she made her way to the airlock. She tore off her suit and put on the only one available. It didn't fit well, but she didn't have a choice. Her only hope was that the seal would hold long enough for her to get to safety.

She waited for what felt like an eternity for the pressurized doors to open. The gunpowder smell of the lunar surface filled her nostrils as she started to run towards the vehicle garage. Much to her horror, the vehicles had been damaged to the point that they weren't drivable.

"Fuck!"

Without any other options, Alana started to run towards Armstrong Base. She had made it a few hundred feet before a sudden jolt from behind caused her to faceplant into the ground. *What the hell was that?* She thought. Alana looked back to see a portion of Aldrin Base was now blown out, with debris floating everywhere. She wasn't sure what had happened, but she knew that she had to get out of there as fast as possible. Alana pushed herself up and began to run away once again. She tried not to think of Scott or the fact that her arm was burning horribly under her suit. Alana knew that her only option was to treat it once she got to Armstrong Base.

A familiar voice came over the radio, causing her heart to shudder in fear.

"Alana... I'm coming for you..." Dr. Popov said, before breaking out into more uncontrollable laughter.

1

Harvey could feel the earth beneath his feet as he chased his prey. As he ran through the forest, dodging every branch and tree that got in his way, he was an animal possessed, chasing the rabbit in front of him. Just when it seemed like he was about to catch it, the creature would gain almost supernatural speed and remain out of reach.

Harvey could feel his heart pounding. He didn't know why he wanted the little creature running from him, he just knew that he needed it. He needed to catch it. He needed to conquer it, to devour it. As the rabbit got farther and farther away, Harvey went from running on his bare feet to crawling on all fours. This closed the distance between hunter and prey. Closer, closer, his heartbeat getting stronger and stronger. He could only hear the beat of his heart. As anticipation of his meal grew, Harvey felt his mouth start to water. Closer, closer, until finally, he lunged through the air, tackling the little rabbit and holding it down. The creature kicked wildly, trying to escape its fate. It knew what was coming as Harvey gripped its small body, feeling its ribs start to crack. Just as he was about to break the creature's neck, it looked up at him and opened its mouth to scream.

"Oh, the weather outside is frightful..."

Harvey shot up from his bed, looking around his room as he composed himself after his nightmare. He brought his hand over to the radio to turn off the Christmas music. The clock read 0600 zulu time. The white sheets of his bed were stained in sweat. He started doing his breathing exercises in hopes of steadying his shaking hands or calming his already jackhammering heart. His watch said that he had a heart rate of 132 bpm. *Center yourself.* He heard the voice of Dr. Adler, the team's psychologist back on earth. She worked with the team during their entire three years of training for the Artemis mission. During that time, she had taught the team what she deemed "essential" calming exercises. Harvey closed his eyes and did his best to control his breathing as he slowly inhaled, counting to five before letting out an exaggerated exhale. He completed this exercise a few more times before looking at his watch again. His heart rate was now a brisk 144.

"Oh, for fuck's sake," Harvey said before getting out of bed. He looked up at the top bunk to see if his roommate Mike was awake. By the look of things, Mike was already up and at 'em, probably working out in the gym. Just like the Marine had always done, if he wasn't sleeping, eating, or working then he was in the gym. Their room was tidy for the most part, or at least Mike's stuff was tidy. Harvey, on the other hand, had what he liked to refer to as organized chaos. He knew just where everything was and liked to keep it that way. To the untrained eye, however, his side of the room could be referred to as sloppy. Harvey's books were scattered over his desk in the corner of the room, while Mike's were neatly organized by subject. Unlike Harvey, who liked to bring a bit of personality to the room, Mike enjoyed the basics. He adhered to the belief that if it was something he needed, it would have been issued to him by the military, or in this case, NASA. In fact, the only object that Mike seemed to care about was the framed photo of his family that stood on his desk.

Harvey was getting a late start to his day, but he didn't see that as too big of a deal considering he'd been up late the night before working on the rovers as well as trying and failing to fix HOGAN, who was the bane of Harvey's existence. Harvey was the team's mechanical engineer and computer science guy, which were fancy titles for what Harvey considered to be his real job: a glorified mechanic. Harvey oversaw the maintenance and more often than not, the retrieval of the hundreds of lunar rovers that NASA was using. HOGAN was easily the most expensive and fragile of these machines. His most recent reason for breaking down was because he fell while holding a can of soda for Mike. An android that cost over fifteen million couldn't even hold a can of soda without breaking.

Harvey glided into the hallway of Armstrong Base, which was somehow duller than the room he shared with Mike. The floors were plain white, while the walls and ceiling were a tasteful egg white. The monotony of the corridor was enough to drive someone mad, if not for one exception: the window panel. For the first time in three weeks, it was open. The fact that the window wasn't locked down by the protective security paneling must have meant that the storm was finally over. Harvey never missed an opportunity to look out that window, and this time was no exception. Harvey unceremoniously put his face onto the window and looked at the lunar surface for the first time in weeks. The cold barren waste of the moon stared back at him. Besides a few tracks from the rovers, the surface was bare, and the atmosphere was quiet. As he looked over the horizon, Harvey saw the small blue illumination of Earth staring back at him. He never got tired of seeing home.

Harvey had been stationed at Armstrong Lunar Base for the last four of what was supposed to be a six-month rotation. During that time, he and his teammates had been investigating the different effects of the lunar surface on Earth-born organisms. That was at least the goal of Armstrong Base, which was one of three bases located near Shackleton Crater. There was also Aldrin Base, which was the biggest of the three. Aldrin wasn't managed exclusively by NASA. Instead, it had been created as a sort of partnership between NASA and the Kronos Organization. Kronos was, by and large, the most successful of the private space firms, due to their wild yet innovative ideas about renewable energy. The third lunar base was the Collins Communication Array. It was slightly farther away from Armstrong and Aldrin base. The Collins team spent their time investigating sound waves in space. Although there wasn't a team at Collins base during this rotation, Harvey had still had to do some maintenance on their rovers. Even when stuff wasn't being used, the moon found a way to break it down.

Harvey entered the gym, only to see Mike, who looked like he had been working out for quite some time. Harvey looked at the machine's screen an almost gasped. If they had still been on earth, then Mike would have been attempting to lift well over 600lbs. Lucky for them, the moon only had one-sixth of Earth's gravity.

"Harvey, nice of you to join us," Mike said in between sets, his tone not changing whatsoever, despite the weight on the bar.

"What do you mean, us?" Harvey asked.

"He means that you overslept for this morning's workout, sugar tits."

Harvey turned to see Jessica Peoples, the Armstrong team's resident botanist. Jessica had just finished running on the treadmill and was undoing the gravity bands tied to her belt. The bands simulated Earth's gravitational pull on the human body and helped astronauts stay fit. One of the biggest challenges mankind had faced since coming to the moon (and space as a whole) had been the long-term effects of gravity—or the lack thereof—on the human body. This is one of the reasons that NASA and Kronos invested billions in what must've been the goofiest-looking workout equipment known to man. It was also the reason that the team had to work out for at least an hour a day. Otherwise, they would lose both muscle mass and bone density.

Harvey put his hands over his chest. "Hey! Quit staring at them!"

"Whatever," said Jessica. "I'm done anyway. I'm just surprised that you weren't up earlier, given that today's the day of the big game. Isn't this one the tiebreaker?"

Jessica was right. Today was the day that Harvey's alma mater, the University of Michigan, played against the Ohio State Buckeyes, which just so happened to be Mike's school. The two schools had what could only be described in the nicest of ways as a heated rivalry. The same could not be said about Mike and Harvey, however, who were, for the most part, the best of friends. The two men had bonded when their astronaut training started just a couple of years ago. Over that time, the two schools had played twice, with each school getting a victory over the other. This game would be the rubber match for the two and the one that determined the winner of a very expensive bottle of whiskey that had been put up for grabs. Mike and Harvey got along fine enough every other day, but on game day, they took great pleasure in talking shit to each another. Jessica, who was a neutral party during this whole exchange, took great pleasure in riling both of them up.

"It's not my fault," said Harvey. "I was up late trying to fix HOGAN again. The stupid piece of shit can drive an LTV, but he can't bring you a soda from the fridge without falling down."

Jessica continued to walk away. "Whatever, I don't care who wins either way. I'm a Ducks fan. Go red and yellow, or something..." she said as she threw up a peace sign and walked out of the room.

"I am surprised that you slept in," said Mike, who had just finished his workout. "I thought for sure you'd be up early planning some elaborate prank for the game. You must have really been tired. Were you chasing rabbits again?"

"You know, I don't appreciate you making fun of my dreams, Mike. I trusted you in confidence with that information and made you swear as a gentleman."

"Oh, that was your first mistake. I'm not a gentleman. I'm a Marine," Mike retorted.

"*I'm-uh-Marine*," Harvey repeated mockingly.

"Aren't you going to work out?" asked Mike.

"Well, I was, but like you said, I'm getting a late start, and break-fast sounds pretty damn good right now. I think that we should get some food in us and then try and knock out whatever tasks we have for the day. That way we can sit down in time for the game," Harvey said.

"I'm all for getting everything done early, but if Commander Sanders hears you haven't been keeping up with your workouts again, she is going to make you work out with her, and that's not something I would wish on my worst enemy."

The Armstrong team was made up mostly civilians, with Mike and Commander Sanders being the only two active-duty military. On top of being a Marine, Mike was a well accomplished Geologist. Of course, this didn't stop Harvey from teasing his friend about eating crayons or any other Marine related insults he found online. Mike and Harvey left the gym and made their way down the corridor. The two men entered the dining room, if you could call it that. The hall, like everything else on Armstrong Base, was illuminated in white. It had one long table for the group to eat at. There was sufficient cabinet space and a freezer that housed all of the team's meals. With the constant rotations that NASA had its astronauts doing, there was enough food on the base to last five years, if needed.

The two men saw Dr. Sanjay Bailey already seated at the table. Sanjay was the resident medical doctor and biologist at Armstrong. Sanjay gave them a nod in recognition. At just twenty-six, Bailey was already very accomplished even before being selected for the Artemis mission. He had graduated from Johns Hopkins at eighteen and went on to work with Doctors without Borders. He soon found himself in Africa, where he battled the Ebola virus. After spending a few years there, he came back to the States and began working for the CDC. At just twenty-three, Sanjay had accomplished more than most doctors would in their entire career. He could have easily coasted the rest of his career, but that wasn't how he was wired. Sanjay had always been a nerd at heart and before he dreamed of helping people, he dreamed of becoming an astronaut. So, when an opportunity with NASA presented itself, Sanjay jumped at the chance. Unfortunately, he soon realized that he was out of his element.

Despite all his accomplishments, Sanjay was lacking in people skills. In fact, one of the issues that the team had early on in training was getting Sanjay to open up. It was actually Harvey, of all people, who was able to get him to start talking and working better with the team. It had started with a simple enough question.

"Hey, do you like anime?"

Harvey had asked this one night after a particularly rough EVA training session in the pool. It was the opening that Sanjay needed to open up to his teammates, and the two men had started bonding over their love of all things *Dragon Ball*, *Attack on Titan*, and *Evangelion*— although they had differing opinions on the last one. Harvey was able to push Sanjay a little bit to come out of his shell, and he soon found common interests with the rest of the team. Like Mike, he also rooted for horrible teams like the Pittsburg Penguins. Sanjay and Jessica bonded over their interest in collecting bugs, while he and the commander debated philosophy. He even found a way to get along with Dr. Holstrom, which was a feat that no one else had managed. After three years with these people, Sanjay had started to come out of his shell, and it was all thanks to Harvey asking him about Japanese cartoons.

The two men went over to the food station and grabbed their items of choice before sitting at the table with Sanjay. "You know, you would think that NASA would have found a better way to give us food up here than putting everything into these vacuum-sealed pouches," Harvey said as he struggled to get his food—a luscious cheeseburger bowl—out of the bag.

"Well, it's not that hard as long as you have muscles, big guy," said Mike, whose joke caused Sanjay to smile in agreement.

As Harvey struggled to open his pouch of food, a sudden alarm blared through the room. The alarm caused Harvey to jolt, ripping the bag and spraying soggy hamburger meat all over himself. Normally, Mike and Sanjay would be laughing their asses off at Harvey's expense, but whenever Commander Sanders started talking, it demanded the team's full attention. "Attention team, this is Sanders. I need you to report to the command center immediately. This is not a drill. Get here. Over and out."

Mike and Sanjay wasted no time getting up from their seats, leaving Harvey to wallow in his self-pity. "Is it too much for me just to enjoy my breakfast?" Harvey exclaimed, chasing after his teammates.

2

Harvey, now covered in bits of cheesy meat, walked into the command center. As usual, he was the last member of the team to arrive. Stepping in awkwardly, he took his seat between Mike and Jessica. Jessica had already changed from her gym clothes. From her wet hair, Harvey guessed she was in the middle of a shower when she heard the commander's call. "What happened to—" Jessica started, only for Harvey to cut her off.

"I don't want to talk about it."

Sanjay smirked as he sat down. He was sitting next to Dr. Gregory Holstrom, the team's chemist. Seated at the head of the table was the team's leader, Lieutenant Colonel Samantha Sanders. Although everyone just called her Commander. This was a nickname that stuck in training when Harvey compared her to a Starfleet Commander. At first, she'd hated the nickname and its lack of formality. Over time, she had come to view it as a form of acceptance from the rest of the crew. Harvey wasn't sure if she still hated it or not, but at the very least, she stopped correcting people when they used it.

At first glance, there was nothing physically significant about Sanders. She was a middle-aged woman of average height with greying blonde hair. Even though she was in great physical shape, she certainly didn't look like she was a super athlete. What separated the commander from everyone else on the team was her stone-cold presence. She had a confidence about her that carried over into everything she did, and this silently motivated those around her. Unlike most career officers, she was open to criticism, but she gave very little to be criticized. Her dependability was established early on in their training with the only opposition coming from the man sitting to her right: Dr. Gregory Holstrom.

Dr. Holstrom was originally projected to be the commander of this mission due to his impressive scientific background and the fact that he was also a former colleague of Allen Burton, the CEO of Kronos. However, Dr. Holstrom proved to be a less than capable leader. The man was a rockstar when it came to chemistry and certainly good at taking care of himself, but when it came to being a leader, he left much to be desired. He acted like more of a self-serving dictator then an actual leader. His people skills were abysmal at best, creating more problems than actual solutions for the team. Even when NASA made the call to replace him as team lead, he was quick to blame the rest of the crew for his failures rather than take responsibility.

Commander Sanders, on the other hand, motivated her people by example. The woman was fourth-generation military—her parents were a retired Army general and Navy admiral, respectively. She was the only child from what could only be described as a tumultuous relationship. At the age of eighteen, she enlisted in the Air Force against her parents' wishes. They wanted her to go to college and pursue something outside of the military, or at the very least finish her degree so she could commission. That path was fine for some, but not for the commander. She knew that if her end goal was to lead airmen, then she wanted to be on the front lines with them, facing hardships together. She had seen how both her parents treated the enlisted force. They might get the job done on paper, but their troops always suffered because of it. She was intent on not being that type of a leader.

The commander spent a few years as an enlisted member of the Air Force before finally getting her degree and commissioning as a fighter pilot. After spending some time on the front lines, she eventually met her husband and together, they had three children. No one would've faulted Commander Sanders for slowing down at that point and transitioning into the cushy position of a squadron commander, but that wasn't for her. She wanted to keep flying and chasing after the next challenge. She knew that she was better suited making decisions in the field rather than behind a desk.

So when the opportunity arose, she transitioned from the Air Force into an experimental pilot position with NASA. This opened doors for her to eventually get onto the Artemis team where she became the first woman to command an expedition. Unlike Dr. Holstrom, Sanders was always open to her team's suggestions. She would hear her people out and take their concerns to heart, but everyone knew that once her decision was made, it was final. That was the biggest difference between the commander and Dr. Holstrom. Well, that and the fact that Harvey was pretty certain Dr. Holstrom enjoyed the smell of his own farts.

"Thank you, everyone, for getting here so quickly. I apologize for the abruptness, I'm sure some of you were in the middle of important tasks. Whether you were showering, working out, or playing with your food…" The commander's gaze fixed on Harvey. "Dr. Holstrom received some good news from the sensors this morning. It looks like the solar storm has finally passed. Now all we need to do is go out there and see what type of damage was done."

This was a common occurrence, given the moon's exosphere was about ten trillion times less dense than the Earth's. This left the lunar surface susceptible to some of space's most deadly natural occurrences. The deadliest two of these space phenomena was the constant threat of being peppered by asteroids or a random solar flare created by the sun. When these flares happened, they could create powerful amounts of radiation. Luckily, the lunar bases protected their crew from such radiation, but the same could not be said about all of the equipment outside. "As you may have guessed, we have lost most of our comms with Gateway and haven't been able to contact Aldrin Base in weeks. We received comms from Gateway this morning, but still no word from Aldrin Base. Any request sent by us or the Gateway crew doesn't go through."

Gateway was the codename for the orbiting lunar station. It served as a midway point for anyone coming and going from the moon. Before astronauts could land on the lunar surface, they would take a shuttle off Earth and dock with Gateway. They would then get onto a differently-configured shuttle to be safely transported to the lunar surface. That same shuttle would then take the old crew up into Gateway and send them back to Earth. It was tedious, but the amount of money that NASA saved by reusing shuttles was astronomical and worth the time spent ping-ponging from point to point. "We're still getting text messages from Gateway and from Vince over at NASA, but we need the communications arrays fixed so that we can get back our instant video messaging and live feeds, and that is coming from Vince himself, so I don't want to hear any sass about it." Sanders looked at Harvey again.

Vince Notley was an accomplished astronaut and one of the pioneers of getting the Artemis program off the ground. The man had flown in five missions and had spent a collective three years in space. Now he'd transitioned from an astronaut to a mission coordinator. He was the only person that Commander Sanders would take any orders from. Vince had earned the crew's respect early on when he went to bat for them over Dr. Holstrom's shortcomings as a leader. In fact, it was him that urged NASA to appoint Commander Sanders to the leadership role rather than rotating the team out altogether.

"Shit..." mumbled Harvey.

The commander heard Harvey's complaint, but Sanjay raised his hand before she could say anything. "Go ahead, Sanjay. I keep telling you, you don't have to raise your hand."

Sanjay sheepishly lowered his arm before starting his question. "Commander, wouldn't it just be better for Aldrin Base to send one of their communications techs out there? The communication array is closer to them, and I'm sure everyone has work to catch up on after being locked down for a few weeks."

"You're absolutely right, Sanjay. It would make more sense for Aldrin Base to fix their own comms, but Vince is worried. He is asking us to take a look at their equipment and do a little welfare

check. Besides, that is only one part of what I need you to do..."
Sanders fixed her gaze on Harvey again.

"What?" asked Harvey, already knowing he wasn't going to like
the answer.

"NASA wants us to take HOGAN—"

"Nope!" interrupted Harvey.

"Let me finish..." continued the commander, barely able to
control her grin. "NASA wants us to take HOGAN and get a
Christmas photo with him for the press."

"Nope!" Harvey protested.

"Harvey!" said Jessica.

"Nope, absolutely fucking not!"

When the Artemis program had started back up, NASA first sent
rovers to the lunar surface and had them start preparing different
sites for the astronauts. Hell, even the very base that they were sitting
in was thanks to rovers. Originally, the bases were little more than
inflatable pods. These pods were meant to be used as a Kevlar-like
insulation to protect the team from the surface. The rovers then went
around the inflated structure and used the materials available on the
moon to 3D print a cocoon around the pods. By Harvey's estimate,
there were 368 rovers on the lunar surface, and he had been respon-
sible for all of them during these last few months. These machines
were one of mankind's most impressive feats of imagination, but to
Harvey, they were just a pain in the ass. Many of the rovers were self-
preserving, handled mostly by their automated functions. Despite
this, the machines were constantly breaking, either because of their
own clumsiness or the many environmental hazards they faced. They
flipped over, fell into craters, and sometimes even got tangled up with
each other while doing the same task. NASA was so proud of showing
off these rovers, but Harvey saw them as just stupid little Roombas.

None of these machines, however, were as big of a pain in the ass
as HOGAN, also known as the Humanoid Orbital Galactic Android.
HOGAN was a science project that NASA was convinced would one
day replace astronauts. The android was meant to have a virtual real-
ity-like interface that allowed astronauts to control it with a visor and
special haptic suit. HOGAN was designed to function in the most

extreme of environments, or at least that was what the scientists liked to remind Harvey every time the android broke down. The damn thing wasn't even an android. He was definitely humanoid in appearance and walked on two legs, and if you put some clothes and a mask on him then he might pass for a mannequin, but otherwise, he had a blank white face that served as a loose form of communication. Emoticon lights would flash on the face to indicate when HOGAN was either completing a task, downloading information, recharging his batteries, or needed repairs.

Harvey and Mike had only formed an attachment to HOGAN because he was able to imitate their most vulgar of gestures when they were wearing the haptic suits, something that they'd found hilarious at first. They named him HOGAN after Hulk Hogan, Mike's favorite wrestler. This was after a NASA scientist showed him doing the classic muscle flex from the Hulkster. Over the last four months, however, HOGAN had proved to be one of the most expensive pains in the ass for this whole mission. But to NASA and the people back on earth, they couldn't get enough of HOGAN. They wanted him to be included in every single update and briefing to the press.

"Didn't we just fuckin' do this, Commander? We dressed him up for Halloween, didn't we?" Harvey cried.

"Yeah, NASA wasn't too thrilled with that, though."

"What do you mean they weren't too thrilled with it? He was a ghost."

"Some people weren't too happy about the ghost costume," Jessica pointed out.

"We are on the moon. A bed sheet is the best we could do. If NASA wanted him to have a better costume, then they should've sent one!"

"Regardless, they just want a simple picture of HOGAN helping you guys put Christmas lights around the communications satellite and it just so happens that we have to go out and do maintenance on it anyway," the commander interjected.

"Commander please, I swear to God, if you make me do this, I'm going to make HOGAN do something extremely vulgar. Okay? I don't want to do it, but you're not leaving me a lot of options here."

"Ohhh, you could always have his face visor spell out the word 'boobs'," said Sanjay.

"Or have him making a jerking-off motion," added Jessica.

"Enough! Sanjay, Jessica, stop encouraging him! And you, Harvey, are going to get me this damn Christmas photo and it's going to be jolly as all hell, am I clear?" the commander ordered.

Harvey was going to continue before Mike put a hand on his shoulder. "Don't worry, ma'am, we'll get it done."

"Thank you, Mike, I appreciate that. The rest of us are going to get suited up and check the structural integrity of the base so we can make sure that nothing else was damaged during the storm. You all are dismissed."

"Have fun, you two," Jessica said as she walked away.

"I hate this place," said Harvey.

Mike replied, "I know, buddy, me too. But hey, look on the bright side, maybe we can get HOGAN to flip off the camera when we take the picture."

3

Harvey handed a set of Christmas lights to HOGAN, who was already sitting in the back seat of the LTV—or lunar terrain vehicle. "Here you go, jackass, hold onto these." HOGAN's hands gripped the lights and his screen showed a smiley face.

σ(^●^)

Thank God HOGAN never realized when he was being insulted.

"All right, that should be about everything. We all good to go with HOGAN?" Mike asked as he finished loading the back of the LTV.

"As good as we can be. I really hope he doesn't break down again out there. I don't want to carry his five-hundred-pound ass back to base," Harvey replied.

"He's not that bad, and besides, he's only eighty-three pounds up here." Mike strapped himself into the driver's seat.

"As long as we can get this done and be back in time for the game, that's all I really care about," Harvey replied as he finished fastening himself into the passenger seat.

"Good point," Mike agreed before keying up his headset. "Greg, are you there?"

"Yes! Dr. Holstrom is here, and yes, I read you just fine, thank you," Dr. Holstrom responded, annoyingly.

"Great! Can you open up the bay door so we can go ahead and get out of here?"

"Have you done all of your proper safety checks?"

Mike rolled his eyes. "Yep, everything."

"Really? You've checked the tire pressure, power steering, and the communications display already? I would like to remind you that you won't be able to hear me once you get a few feet from base. I would hate for you to need me to come rescue..." continued Dr. Holstrom.

"Greg, open the fucking door," Harvey snapped. Dr. Holstrom was perhaps the least-liked member of Armstrong Base. He wasn't necessarily a bad person, but he did walk around with a sense of superiority to everyone that he interacted with. That character trait had been a key factor in leading to the team's friction and Holstrom's removal as lead. Although he seemed to have gotten over it in recent months, the wound to his pride is still there—not that he would admit it aloud, but it showed in how unnecessarily particular he was when discussing tasks with team members. On more than one occasion, Harvey had seen Dr. Holstrom directing Jessica on how to better store her plants or explaining to Mike the intricacies of the rock samples they had taken. It would be one thing if Dr. Holstrom was talking to an average person, but he is talking to respected specialists in their fields. Truthfully, Harvey wasn't sure if Dr. Holstrom saw a difference. In his mind, everyone but him was an idiot. When it wasn't a mandatory meeting or group activity, the doctor spent most of his time in his room. He was the only member of the team that still had their own room for some reason, which also rubbed everyone the wrong way.

As the doors opened from the garage, Mike started up the LTV and the two men drove out onto the lunar surface. The smell of gunpowder hit Harvey's nostrils as they exited the garage and drove off at a brisk 25 miles an hour. "When we get to the display, I'm going to need your help with taking a few samples. That damned storm cut into valuable research time on the surface," Mike said. The fact that Mike was a geologist, was the main reason he had been recruited by

NASA. Should anything happen to Commander Sanders, he was also the team's backup pilot.

"No problem," said Harvey. "Let's rock."

"Harvey, that joke wasn't funny the first week of training and it isn't funny now three years later."

"Says you," retorted Harvey.

During the day, the moon would reach temperatures of 127°C, and at night, -173°C. The lowest temperature experienced on Earth was in the Antarctic at just -89°C. When the original astronauts came to the moon, it was during the lunar dawn, which was considered the sweet spot for getting work done outside. High noon on the moon starts every seven days, and sunset begins at fourteen. Nighttime could last for two weeks. This was what made dawn and dusk the best time for any work outside of the base, but it only gave the team a little over a month total out of the whole six-month rotation to get any actual work done. Due to the severe solar flare, the team has lost two of the seven days that they'd originally planned for outside work. Today was a 'catch-up day.'

The two men were soon out of Armstrong Base's communication range. Until Harvey started his repairs, they would be unable to contact anyone. Harvey was messing around with his wrist computer when he heard Mike whistle at something.

"Damn! Hard to believe we will be getting on that thing in just a couple of months. Where has the time gone?"

Harvey looked over to the large shuttle that stood a few hundred feet away. The shuttle was the largest vehicle on the lunar surface, and both crews would be using it to leave the moon in the next couple of months. From there, they would rendezvous with Gateway before returning to Earth. The lunar shuttle was strategically placed between both Aldrin and Armstrong, serving as a midway point.

"Level with me here, Mike. How many samples do you have to take today?"

"Technically?"

"Yeah, technically."

"Upwards of thirty-six."

"Fuck!" said Harvey.

"But...considering today is game-day and that bottle of Johnny Blue is on the line... I'd say that we can narrow that down to about six and catch up the next day."

"Mike, I like the way you think."

Mike and Harvey spent the next hour checking the different communication arrays around base, with a few stops in-between for Mike to take samples. Each time the pair stopped, they checked with Dr. Holstrom to see if anyone had gotten a hold of Aldrin Base yet. Each time, he informed them that they hadn't had any luck. After an hour of repairs and specimen collection, the pair finally made their way to the last station. This station was furthest out and nearest to Aldrin.

The drive only took them ten minutes, but for Mike, it felt like an hour with Harvey's bad attitude.

"Look, all I'm saying is that I think it's bullshit that we have to come all the way out here and fix their shit. I mean, at what point are Simmons or the rest of their crew going to get their shit together and learn how to fix their own comms? It's not hard. You replace the solar panels, you flip a few switches, and boom! Communications display fixed. But no, every time one of these things go out, it has to be me to fix it. We've already checked five arrays, Mike. FIVE! There's no reason they shouldn't be able to talk to us."

"Well, either way, we'll get this one going and see if that fixes anything. You go ahead and do what you got to do. I'll get HOGAN set up."

"All right, fine, but if this doesn't fix it, then we need to do some serious remedial training with those guys," Harvey groused as he disembarked the LTV to start working on the communications array. At this point, fixing the array had become muscle memory. Harvey was sure that he could even fix them with his eyes closed, but he didn't dare try. He tried it with the base's coffeemaker a couple of months ago, and it had worked well enough at first—until it shot coffee at the crew instead of their cups. Harvey would have been able to fix it too if Dr. Holstrom hadn't tattled on him to the commander. She made sure that he didn't try to fix anything blindfolded ever again.

As Harvey replaced the solar panels, Mike was behind him getting HOGAN set up for the picture. "You know, I can't wait for us to eventually get a decent version of HOGAN here that can go out and do all of our work for us without constantly losing their footing or breaking our tools in the process," Harvey said.

"Oh, come on. HOGAN's not that bad. I think that if you just knew how to handle him better, he wouldn't have so many issues. Besides, look at how he looks with his little Santa hat on," Mike said as he placed the hat on HOGAN's egg-shaped head. "Besides, if he wasn't having so many issues, then I think you'd be out of a job bud."

"No way! Even if they could get somebody with my expertise, they can't match my looks. Don't forget, I'm the eye candy of this team." Harvey screwed the panel shut and flipped a few switches. "And that should just about do it." He flipped the final switch and it instantly powered up. The circular dish on its antenna started to rotate, indicating that it was working properly.

"Good job, Harvey. Now here, hold these lights and make it look like you two are having fun. I'll go set up the camera." Mike shoved a string of Christmas lights in Harvey's arms. The other end was held by HOGAN.

"HOGAN, be happy," Harvey said.

$$(/ \wedge \_ \wedge)/$$

HOGAN was programmed to respond to different words using his emoticons. "Be happy" was one of thirty different expressions that he was able to exhibit.

"Perfect," said Mike, who had just finished setting up the camera.

The two men and HOGAN each held up a strand of Christmas lights with HOGAN looking like he was laughing. The three looked like they were decorating the communications array like a Christmas tree.

"How long do we have to hold this?" Harvey asked.

"It's on a timer. It's taking a few shots right now. I'm going to send it back to NASA and they can figure out which one they like best."

"Perfect, so we are done?" asked Harvey

"Should be."

"Okay, let's just get one more. HOGAN, suck it," Harvey said.

HOGAN suddenly dropped the lights and made a chopping gesture toward his crotch. The emoticon on his face turned from a smiley face to an angry face.

ᕙ(ò_óˇ)ᕗ

Mike started laughing, and Harvey gave the camera the middle finger.

"That's great. I got to see how that looks," Mike said, dropping his lights and walking toward the camera.

"Hey, wait for me!" Harvey called, also dropping his lights and hurrying toward Mike. The picture showed HOGAN chopping at his crotch in all his glory. It was everything the two men could have hoped for.

"I'm sending this to my own email. I don't care what photo NASA uses, but this is going to be my own Christmas card. I'm gonna send it to my parents. They'll love it," Harvey laughed, as HOGAN continued to chop at his crotch.

"What is that?" Mike asked suddenly, pointing at a red dot in the background of the picture.

"I don't know," said Harvey, "but it's in the other ones too..."

"And it looks like it's getting closer." The two men looked up to the horizon.

Past the crotch-chopping HOGAN, they saw a red figure running toward them. "Who the fuck is that?" Harvey exclaimed.

"It's gotta be one of Aldrin crew. They should be able to hear us now that the communications are back, right?" Mike asked.

"As long as they have their radio on," Harvey replied.

Both men switched over to the general frequency in their EVA suit. Each suit had a channelizer that allowed different teams to communicate with each other. Mike and Harvey have been using their own personal frequency because of the range. The general frequency was normally active when the communication arrays were working properly, which allowed for members of each base to communicate with each other.

"This is Major Michael Murdock. Whoever is running toward us at the communications array, identify yourself," Mike said sternly, the Marine in him taking over.

The crimson astronaut said nothing. The only sound they heard was the astronaut's labored breathing.

"Did they get new suits?" Harvey asked. "It looks like that EVA is red."

"I think we're about to find out," Mike replied.

The mystery astronaut was now just a few meters away. Harvey wasn't sure what he should be doing so he looked at Mike. Whether on purpose or by instinct, Mike had taken a defensive posture. The Marine was ready for anything—or almost anything. Both men were shocked when the crimson astronaut, now just twenty feet away, collapsed.

"Shit!"

Without a word, the two men ran toward the fallen astronaut.

"Give me a hand here," Mike asked as he went to turn the astronaut over. He was probably thinking the same thing that Harvey was. Any fall, any tumble, on the lunar surface could mean excruciating death for the clumsy individual. The surface of the moon was made up of some of the hardest igneous rocks known to man. Its jagged surface had been a constant issue for visitors of the lunar environment, because even the slightest scrape was enough to breach an EVA suit.

As the men turned over the crimson astronaut, they immediately noticed the suit's name tape read, "Jackson"

"Colonel Jackson, are you okay, sir?" asked Mike, but he received no answer.

Lt. Colonel Jackson was the team lead for Aldrin Base. "Colonel Jackson, it's Murdoch and Howlett from Armstrong, are you hurt?" Mike continued.

"Lift his solar shield. He might not be conscious," Harvey suggested.

Mike lifted the golden visor up from Jackson's helmet only to reveal that it wasn't Jackson at all. Instead, the men were greeted by the blank face of Dr. Alana Chang—the accomplished chemist who worked closely with Dr. Popov.

As Mike moved the solar shield, Harvey noticed that the crimson wasn't the suit. He looked over the doctor and saw that some of the red stain on her EVA had been wiped away from the fall.

"Mike, what is this stuff?" Harvey asked, looking for some sort of assurance it wasn't what he thought it was. He received no such assurance.

"It's blood, Harvey…"

"Blood? But where is she bleeding from?"

"It's not hers!"

"Well then, whose is it?"

Mike didn't say anything. He just examined Dr. Chang, his combat training taking over. "Dr. Chang, can you hear me? Dr. Chang? It's okay. You're with Mike and Harvey from Armstrong Base. Do you remember us? Dr. Chang?"

The doctor had a glazed look in her eye. She was breathing heavily, and she was definitely conscious, but she wouldn't—or couldn't— look at either one of them.

"Lycaon," she whispered.

"Lysol? Did she say Lysol?" Harvey asked.

Suddenly, Dr. Chang sat up and grabbed Harvey tightly. Tighter than he thought the short, slender doctor would be capable of. She looked him directly in the eye.

"LYYYYCAAAONNNN!" she growled before she began to weep, tears streaming down her face. The power in her grip had disappeared entirely as she collapsed back to the ground.

"Lycaon, Lycaon, Lycaon, Lycaon, Lycaon…" she continued to yell franticly as she thrashed. Then, as quickly as she'd come to life, Dr. Chang slipped into unconsciousness. Harvey looked at Mike for guidance, but he looked just as confused as Harvey.

"Get a hold of Armstrong and get HOGAN. I'll get her loaded into the LTV."

Harvey stood and switched over to the Armstrong frequency as he made his way to HOGAN. "Commander, it's Harvey. Do you read me?"

"Oh, Harvey. Good, you got the communications display working. The commander is still out checking the base integrity. What can I help you with?"

"Greg, there's been an accident. Dr. Chang is here. We think that she was attacked," Harvey explained.

Greg's cocky tone changed immediately to pure panic. "What? Attacked, by who? By what?"

Harvey looked down at Mike as he picked up Dr. Chang before scanning the rest of the horizon. He didn't see anything, not a soul in sight, yet he couldn't help feeling like he was being watched.

"I have no idea..."

4

Mike entered the passcode and initiated the body scan. Each base had an EVA scanner and cipher lock with a passcode. The scanners were less for security and more of a way to keep track of who was in and out of the facility. Every time someone entered or exited, their suit was scanned and logged into the system. This way, the crew—and NASA—knew what time someone entered or exited the base. Harvey and Mike carried Dr. Chang through the depressurization station and waited a few seconds while it acclimated to the base's pressure. After the door panel shifted from a red light to a green one, it slid open. Harvey pushed it to open quicker.

Mike was carrying Dr. Chang. All three still had on their EVA suits, helmets included. Sanders was waiting for them. "Is she responsive?" the commander asked.

"No. She passed out a few minutes ago," answered Harvey.

"Okay. Get her to Sanjay, quick," said the commander, and the four of them hurried down the corridor. The group made it to the medical bay in a matter of seconds, where Sanjay and Jessica were already waiting for them.

"Drop her on the gurney. Set her down gently, Mike. We're not sure what type of injuries she has," Sanjay said. He was already dressed in a gown and appropriate PPE.

As Mike set Dr. Chang on the table, Sanjay turned to Harvey. "Okay. Walk me through it one more time. Was there any leak in her suit? Did you see any injuries, either external or internal?"

"No. Nothing," Harvey replied. "We... We don't think it's her blood. She has some scrapes on her face, but that's the only injury we noticed. Her suit was reading normal as far as air supply went. We kept everything on, though, just to be on the safe side." Sanjay turned his full attention to Dr. Chang. "Okay, that's good. You guys did good!" He glanced at Jessica, who was setting up the defibrillator. "I need you to help me get this suit off so we can check for injuries."

"Already doing it," Jessica said.

As a botanist, Jessica had been sent to Armstrong Base because it was the only lunar base with a greenhouse attached. Her job was to study the effects of gravity, or the lack thereof, on plant growth.

Unfortunately for Jessica, the greenhouse had been struck by a meteorite just three months into the rotation and almost every single plant she'd been studying had been destroyed. She had a few specimens tucked away in the base, but her primary mission had been to study the greenhouse plants. Those plants had been on the lunar surface since the last mission, and their survival could have had huge implications for future missions. In a lot of ways, it was seen as a gateway of sorts to establishing a colony.

While she was still doing her best to examine the other plants, much of her workload had decreased without the greenhouse. Most people would've probably wallowed in self-pity, but as adaptive as Jessica was, she started helping everyone else with their tasks. She assisted Sanjay with his tests, Commander Sanders with maintaining records, Mike in collecting rock samples, and Dr. Holstrom with his work when he wasn't being a complete ass. She would even help Harvey with repairing the rovers—if you could call it help. Really, she just sat in the garage and heckled him while occasionally handing him tools. He was perfectly fine with that, though. Truth be told, he liked having her around. She challenged him like no one had before and he enjoyed that in a kind of demented way. Harvey felt like there might be something more between the two, but he knew neither would act on it during the rotation. NASA was pretty adamant about the many dangers of hooking up in space. Still, looking at her now amid the chaos, Harvey couldn't help but admire her.

"Hey, asshats, I need you to step into the hall. It's getting cramped in here," Jessica ordered them.

God, I love her, Harvey thought.

Sanders started to question Harvey and Mike as they took off their EVA suits. "What was it that she said to you? What word?"

Sanjay and Jessica were cutting the EVA suit from Dr. Chang. "Hold on one second," Jessica said. "I think I found an injury." She had stopped cutting the suit's sleeve because she had found what appeared to be scratch marks on the doctor's forearm.

"Those are deep," said Sanjay. "Definite lacerations, but I'm not sure if that explains all of the blood on her suit."

As soon as Sanjay touched the doctor's wound, Chang's eyes shot open. The doctor's sudden consciousness shocked the pair of would-be healers so much that they both took a step back.

"Dr. Chang?" Sanjay asked nervously. "It's okay. You're at Armstrong Base. It's me... Dr. Bailey? Do you rememb—"

If Dr. Chang remembered, she gave no indication. Instead, she began to scream. Sanjay instinctually stepped toward her, and the good doctor was kicked in the gut for his troubles and with enough force to send him flying across the room. Dr. Chang sat up from the gurney and grabbed Jessica by the neck and face. She pulled Jessica until their faces were practically touching, still screaming as she did. For a second, it looked like Dr. Chang was going to bite her. Luckily, Mike was there to help. The Marine jumped into the fray, grabbing the doctor from behind in a type of headlock.

"Let her go, Alana," he ordered her. To her credit, Dr. Chang listened, but only for her to instead focus on Mike.

As the five-foot-five, 140-pound Dr. Chang sprang from the gurney, the 6'2", 200-pound Mike did his best to keep control, but the woman's violent squirming allowed her to break free. Harvey ran toward the pair so he could help. Before he could even figure out what to do, however, he was met with a small fist to the jaw that sent him spiraling to the ground.

Harvey had been punched twice in his life. Once when he was

seven, by his older sister Jenny in retaliation for his melting some of her Barbies with a magnifying glass. The other time was when Harvey and his robotics team decided to celebrate their victory over Michigan State. They went to a local pub, and after having one too many pina coladas, Harvey had mouthed off to one of the bouncers. Harvey guessed that the big man only punched him at half-strength, but it was still enough for him to wake up the next day with a stiff jaw and a horrible headache.

Dr. Chang had punched him harder than either of those times. Instinct took over and Harvey tried to stand, but his legs were not cooperating. As he looked around the room, Mike and Jessica were both trying to wrestle Dr. Chang, who was still screaming and acting like a wild animal. She was able to kick Jessica back to the ground and looked like she was going to pounce on her if not for Mike jumping in again. Mike grabbed Dr. Chang once more but the doctor, seemingly getting stronger by the second, was able to get free by elbowing him in the gut.

"Dr. Chang," came a voice behind Harvey.

The doctor turned, and Sanders punched her square in the face. This seemed to daze the madwoman enough for Sanjay to catch her. For a split-second, it looked like she was about to go back into a berserker rage with her eyes dead-set on the commander. She shook Sanjay off, knocking him to the floor in the process, and began to charge at Commander Sanders. She didn't get very far before something changed abruptly. Dr. Chang gritted her teeth and looked down at Sanjay, and Harvey realized Sanjay had injected the doctor with something when he grabbed her. Chang let out a low growl as her legs started to give out. She tried to steady herself on the gurney before ultimately succumbing.

Dr. Chang was unconscious once more. Sanjay lifted her back onto the table and restrained her with the emergency harness. Everyone was looking around and trying to catch their breath. Harvey was gripping his jaw, moving it slightly to make sure it wasn't broken.

"What the fuck was—" Harvey began before he was cut off by an annoyed Sanders.

"Save it, Harvey." The commander was gripping her wrist, clearly in pain.

"How the hell did it take four of us to restrain her?"

"Adrenaline?" suggested Mike.

"No way! Adrenaline couldn't do all that. Maybe she's on something?" Jessica offered, exasperated.

"Dr. Bailey, do you have any theories?" Sanders asked.

Sanjay raised his hands. "I won't know anything until I at least get a little bit more time with her. The sedative should keep her out for the next few hours, and she should be a little groggy after that. Hopefully, we don't have a repeat of this."

"Either way, she stays strapped onto that goddamn table until we know what the hell is going on, is that clear?"

"Crystal, ma'am," Jessica said, sounding like she'd managed to catch her breath.

"Commander," came Dr. Holstrom's voice over the intercom. "Please report to the command center at your earliest convenience. NASA is on the phone and they have something that you're going to want to see."

5

The crew didn't waste any time filing into the command center. Usually, the commander would be the one to communicate with NASA and relay any orders, but given situation, she felt it best for everyone to know what exactly was going on. Dr. Holstrom was already sitting at the computer when the group—minus Sanjay, who remained with Dr. Chang—walked in.

"Commander, I have Mr. Notley and Lieutenant Colonel Hannon on the video screen for you," Dr. Holstrom said.

Vince Notley was the head of the Artemis program. He was supposed to be on the first Artemis mission back to the lunar surface. Unfortunately for him, a last-minute training injury took him out of the mission. Vince was eventually able to make it back onto the Artemis team. Over an impressive ten-year career, the man has more time on the lunar surface then anyone in history. After retiring from the lunar rotations, he had gone to work at NASA and had been there ever since. After Sanders, Vince was probably the person that the entire crew respected the most. Behind the man's gruff exterior was someone who cared deeply for those around him.

When the crew walked into the command center, Vince's face was already plastered on the screen. The bags under his eyes made Harvey think that he hadn't slept in days. He was smoking a cigarette even though there was clearly a "no smoking allowed" sign on the wall behind him in the mission control room. He was famous for two things: being the smartest person in the room and having one hell of a temper. "Samantha, good, you're here, and you brought the rest of the crew. How is Dr. Chang doing? Has she said anything?" Vince asked.

The commander was still gripping her wrist. "I had to knock her out. Dr. Bailey is monitoring her vitals."

"Did you say 'knocked out'?" asked Vince.

"She didn't leave us with many options, Vince. She was being combative. Hell, even Mike couldn't control her. Dr. Bailey gave her a sedative. Hopefully, she's more cooperative when she wakes up in the next couple of hours. Have you been able to make contact with Aldrin Base?"

"Well, that's actually why I'm calling you. Despite the boys fixing our comms—good job, by the way, fellas—we have been unable to make any contact with Aldrin Base. Colonel Hannon, however, does have something that he needs to share. I thought it would be best that all of us hear it together. Hannon, if you would?"

Lt. Colonel Philip Hannon appeared on the other monitor next to Vince. Hannon was the commander of Gateway, the station acting as the midway point between Earth and the lunar surface.

"Right. Thanks, Vince. Armstrong team, I'm glad to see you are all doing well. As you know, a few days ago, we experienced a pretty significant solar storm, The crews remained within their bases and put up their radiation shields. The storm lasted for a few days and once it was over, we had the unfortunate realization that the majority of our communications networks were knocked out, with the only exception being the ability to send encrypted messages and—"

"Phil! Please hurry this along," said an annoyed Vince. Phil looked nervous, which wasn't like him. Hannon was famous for his carefree attitude. In fact, some would say that he was a little too carefree, but the man had more time in space than anyone in the Artemis program beside Vince, so no one typically questioned him.

"Right, sorry, it's just... It's a lot. The point is that we temporarily lost full communication capabilities with all three lunar bases. Before that happened, however, we received a distress call from Aldrin. We believe it was from Lt. Colonel Jackson, but due to a technical issue, we were only able to receive audio. It's difficult to understand, but it's the only clip we have."

Hannon pressed a button offscreen and the message started to play. The panicked voice of Lt. Col Jackson came over the intercom.

"NASA! This is Lieutenant Colonel Jackson—assistance immediately—changed, all of them—evacuating the mission—" It was hard to make out some parts because there was a lot of static. They couldn't tell if there was someone screaming or crying in the background. Either way, Jackson continued his transmission while clearly trying not to let the panic in his voice impede him. "He's gone insane —immediate evacuation of Aldrin base—help us..."

"Do we have any idea wh—" Mike began, thinking that the transmission was done. His question was cut short when a loud scream erupted over the recording, followed by an explosion.

"That, as far as we can tell, is the end of the transmission," Hannon finished.

"And we haven't heard anything from them since we repaired the communications arrays?" Sanders asked.

Vince and Hannon both stared apprehensively at the crew. Vince finally said something after a few seconds.

"We don't know..."

"You don't know? What does that even..."

Hannon cut Jessica off. "We received another transmission after you were able to fix the communications array, but we're not sure what time it was sent due to the solar storm messing up our systems. In all honesty, we're not even sure if it was sent on purpose or not."

Without saying another word, Hannon pressed a button offscreen once more to start the other transmission. The crew heard what sounded like scraping and grunting. Harvey thought it sounded like someone was struggling to lift something. At first, he thought it might've been one of the crew making noise in the background before the noise suddenly stopped. The silence didn't last long however, because the next thing Harvey and the rest the crew heard sounded like high-pitched squealing before eventually turning into laughter and then turning into a low growl.

"That is the last transmission that we received. We were unfortunately out of rotation during this, so we didn't have eyes on Aldrin Base. We were able to get an image from one of the satellites nearby. This is what they saw."

An image flashed over the screen of an aerial view of the base.

"As you can see, there is significant damage to the integrity of the lab module."

Harvey looked at the screen in disbelief. Aldrin Base was almost double the size of Armstrong. Most of that was because Aldrin had four laboratory modules connected to it while Armstrong only had one. In fact, the four lab modules combined were the same size as all of Armstrong Base. Looking up at the screen, it looked like half of Aldrin's lab modules had exploded.

"Just making sure, is there any chance that this damage could have been caused by the solar storm or a meteor?" Mike asked.

"As far as my crew has been able tell, there is no indication of impact from a meteor, but we can't entirely rule it out."

"From what we're seeing here at mission control, it looks like it was only the laboratory modules that were affected. Aldrin Base as a whole is still functional, but it looks like it's on emergency power. Right now, the best theory is that the damage to the laboratory modules came from inside," Vince said.

"Inside the base? How would that even happen? With all the fail-safes in place, you would almost need to do that much damage on purpose," said Jessica.

Vince took another puff of his cigarette before continuing. His gravelly voice somehow sounded more grim than usual.

"Listen, crew, I'm going to be straight with you. After listening to the recordings and examining some of the other evidence, the most popular hypothesis is that someone may have sabotaged Aldrin Base."

The room was so quiet that for a second, Harvey thought he was standing out in the void of space.

"Based on what we're seeing, the trajectory of the lab debris and the presence of what appears to be fire damage, we think that an explosion occurred within the base. Normally, we would consider this to be a freak accident, but given the nature of the recordings, we worry that it may be something else. As Dr. Peoples said, it is extremely hard to accidently do anything to these bases, let alone blow them up."

"That just seems a bit farfetched. We're only out here on six-month rotations. That's not nearly enough time for someone to go crazy," Dr. Holstrom said.

"Clearly you've never been deployed to the desert," Mike countered.

Dr. Holstrom just looked at him with disdain. "No, I'm not an idiot. Even if someone did lose their marbles over there, there were five other crewmembers. Surely somebody could have gained control of the situation."

Harvey wanted to say something smart-alecky to Dr. Holstrom about how he wouldn't be saying that if he had seen what just transpired with Dr. Chang, but he decided to give his sore jaw a break.

"I don't know why we are jumping straight into sabotage. How do we know that it wasn't just a lab experiment gone wrong?"

"I understand the concern, Dr. Holstrom, and believe me, we are working closely with the people at Kronos to figure out what exactly was in those laboratories, but until we get more information, whether from them or from Dr. Chang, we are left with a limited number of options."

Silence followed once more before Commander Sanders finally spoke up. "What do you want us to do, Vince?"

Vince took another puff of his cigarette before letting out a low sigh. "NASA is electing to evacuate the Artemis mission."

"Bullshit," Harvey said, much louder than what he meant to.

The rest of the team looked at him in shock. Vince only kept the same sullen look on his face.

"Trust me, I feel the exact same way that you do. Which is why I wanted to talk to the team first. NASA wants us to evacuate in order to mitigate any risk to the rest of the team. They don't know what caused the explosion at Aldrin and truth be told, Kronos isn't exactly being very forthcoming with what supplies they had there. I also know that if we evacuate now, we lose any option of helping whoever might still be alive there. I would prefer to wait for Dr. Chang to wake up so that we can get some insight, but time is very clearly of the essence here. Our other option is sending a small team from Armstrong to investigate and potentially rescue the Aldrin crew. Now, I realize that this can seem rather dangerous, but…"

"I'll do it," interrupted Harvey.

"Harvey!" the commander started to cut him off, but he wasn't listening.

"Maybe I can take the base off emergency power and properly assess the equipment. I could get a more accurate report than just a few satellite images."

"If he's going, you should send me too," Mike said. "If Dr. Chang is any indication, then someone will more than likely need some medical attention. I might not be as good as Dr. Bailey, but I'm still pretty decent at stitching up a wound."

"I can help with the first aid too," Jessica put in. "I can have Sanjay prepare a first aid kit for us. Besides, you don't want to send these two girls if there's any heavy lifting involved."

That last comment gave Vince a small chuckle.

"I'm not sure," Sanders began, but Harvey caught her off.

"Ma'am, please. They could still be alive over there. We owe it to them to at least make an effort."

The commander looked at her crew, clearly thinking through her options before answering. She let out a small sigh before turning back to the monitor.

"Well, Vince, it looks like we have our volunteers. Now, we just need a plan."

6

Harvey strapped himself into the passenger seat of the HAB. The HAB—or habitation module rover—was the largest rover available to the Armstrong crew. It was designed for expeditions that required the crew to spend extended periods of time on the lunar surface. The HAB was equipped with an advanced life support system and extra EVA suits in case one of the crew's suits suffered a breach. Armstrong astronauts typically drove the LTV rovers since they were lightweight and easier to maneuver, but the commander thought that the crew should take the HAB in case they encountered anyone from Aldrin Base. Mike was the most capable driver on the team, but even he felt a little overwhelmed driving the HAB. Unlike the LTV, the HAB was clunky and could be a pain in the ass when making tight turns.

Harvey struggled at first to fasten himself into his seat. Harvey's jaw had been stiff since the attack by Dr. Chang a couple of hours ago. He found that doing jaw exercises helped alleviate the pain but not by much.

"Man, she really got you good, huh?" Mike asked jokingly as he sat in the driver's seat.

"Don't give me that shit, man! You know damn well that Dr. Chang was coked up on something. Besides, you two didn't do any better."

Jessica piped up from the back of the rover. "Speak for yourselves! I had her right where I wanted her until Commander Sanders got in the way."

That gave Harvey and Mike a small chuckle.

"I'm sure you did, Jessica. It's just like the commander to make a situation worse," Mike joked. Mike shifted in his chair in an attempt to readjust himself. Harvey saw him wince suddenly and begin to reach toward his chest. Mike must have seen Harvey looking at him because he quickly tried to play it off like he had an itch.

"Hey, man, how are you feeling after that elbow?"

Mike lightly beat his chest. "I've had worse, but not by much. Hopefully she won't be as ferocious when she wakes up next time."

Just like a Marine, trying not to show any signs of weakness. Mike flipped a couple of switches on the front console and the HAB started right up.

"Are ya strapped in back there, Jessica?"

"I'm good. It's pretty spacious back here, and I can't hear Harvey bitching as much, so that's a plus," she answered.

"Lucky you... Commander, this is Mike and the rest of the crew. We are ready for you guys to open her up."

The commander's voice echoed through the intercom in the central console.

"All right, team. Greg is opening up the doors for you. I just wanna double-check that you have all of your gear? Specifically, the first aid kits?"

The rover was built so that the front had a driver and passenger seat while the back of the vehicle had an open space for other passengers and equipment. The whole thing resembled a futuristic garbage truck. Depending on what the mission was, the team could transport a good portion of their equipment within the HAB before having to put it onto the smaller LTVs. The only equipment onboard for this mission, however, was various first aid kits and medicines that Sanjay recommended.

"We are good to go. If anyone needs any help, we will have everything we could need," Jessica replied.

"Except for a gun," Mike muttered.

"Thank you, Captain Murdoch, for that segue into my next reminder. If you find anyone alive at Aldrin Base, exercise extreme caution. We still don't know why Dr. Chang acted the way that she did, but I don't want to risk any further incidents because we were too lackadaisical with people we perceive as our friends. Clearly something happened over there and until we know what that is, I will remind all of you to exercise extreme caution. If you run into any hostility, you are to book it back to the HAB and come back home. I don't want anyone playing the hero here. Is that understood?"

The crew replied "Yes, ma'am!" almost in unison before Mike drove out of the garage.

The first part of the drive was spent mostly in silence, with just the occasional observations about the landscape and what looked to be new craters. On one occasion, Jessica had Mike stop because she thought that she saw some movement, but it turned out to be a small mining rover taking rock samples.

The drive from Armstrong to Aldrin usually took around forty minutes, even though the two bases were only a few miles apart. This was due to the dangerously uneven lunar terrain and the fact that the HAB's max speed was a meager 30 MPH. As the drive continued, Harvey tried on several occasions to start a conversation with Mike and Jessica. He would ask what they thought happened at Aldrin or if they should develop a strategy in case somebody tried to fight them. Neither seemed receptive to his attempts at humor. All he received was one-word answers. One-word answers followed by more silence. Harvey hated the silence, but he understood why everyone was so tense. He assumed they were just as nervous as he was.

Whatever had happened at Aldrin Base, it was unlikely that the rest of the crew was alive. They all knew this was probably a recovery mission, not a rescue. Everyone had so many questions. It was in their nature, most of them were scientists after all. Even Harvey, who considered himself a glorified mechanic, had a need to get to the bottom of any question. It was in their nature, but after seeing Dr. Chang like that, Harvey wasn't sure he wanted these answers.

Every one of them had been put through countless stress tests. Their training made them believe that they could overcome anything.

Any problem, no matter how big or small. They could work and rework it until they found a solution.

Dr. Chang was one of the most mentally tough people Harvey had met since starting his training for the Artemis mission. She grew up in poverty. By the time she was seven, she had lost her father and brother in a Chinese "re-education" camp. When she was ten, she and her mother had immigrated to the United States, but soon after that, her mother died of leukemia. Despite the setbacks, she still worked her ass off, putting herself through school and becoming a respected chemist. By the time she made it into the astronaut program, there wasn't a challenge you could put in front of her that would make her falter. The fact that someone like that could have such an adverse reaction to whatever had happened at Aldrin Base worried the hell out of Harvey.

"We're coming up on Aldrin," Mike reported back to Armstrong Base.

"Roger," acknowledged the commander. Harvey knew she was anxiously watching the video feeds from the HAB and the EVA suits.

Aldrin Base appeared on the horizon. The base was twice the size of Armstrong and not nearly as much of an eyesore. Kronos had clearly spared no expense for this one.

The base had special rovers that were used for cleaning its exterior and were even programed to put on a fresh coat of paint after every crew rotation. Unlike Armstrong Base, which was surrounded by crater-filled terrain, Aldrin's terrain was mostly flat. They also had a large rock formation located two hundred yards south, which looked more like a mountain and reached well over a hundred feet in height. There was a large opening at the base that led to a network of tunnels. Those tunnels had been a part of the natural formation of the moon and something that Kronos had been especially interested in.

Kronos was all about finding and claiming lunar resources. they had even created an impressive "railgun" system capable of firing resources back to Earth. The resources would be placed in a protective container and shot from the Moon to Earth. They had tested it out a few times with mixed success but hadn't had any reason to use it since.

The moon was full of titanium, aluminum, and even uranium, but Kronos wasn't interested in those. They were common enough on Earth and although useful, they weren't a necessity in the lunar environment.

The real reason that Kronos spent most of its resources on digging was their hope of finding ice. Scientists believed that there was once water on the moon. This water, if it still existed, would be in the deeper tunnels. If they could find a large chunk of ice, they could use it to create hydrogen, which could be used to create fuel. Once they had the fuel, they would become the only game in town for any shuttles that need to refuel. While it might not be a big deal immediately, having a fuel source on the moon was an absolute necessity if mankind ever hoped to take a shuttle further than Mars. Luckily—or unluckily, depending on how you looked at it, Kronos hadn't been able to find any ice worth mining in the last decade.

"Mike, don't forget about the panels on your left. We don't wanna park near one and come back to a melted HAB."

"We certainly don't. Thanks for the reminder, Jessica."

Jessica was referring to the large array of solar panels just a few hundred feet away from the base. Kronos rovers had printed the football field length of solar panels onto the lunar surface over the last decade. These panels were the original reason that Kronos decided to get into the space business.

Codenamed Project Firefly, their purpose was to collect large amounts of solar energy that would be converted into microwaves. The panels would then beam the microwaves to collection panels back on Earth, and those panels would convert it into clean energy. Kronos believed that this energy would be able to power a large city for months at a time. Everyone was applauding them for their bold new advances toward clean energy, but the reality was that this invention would make them the biggest clean energy game in town. If these panels proved to be successful, then Kronos would have a monopoly on clean energy technology. They would also control the switch for which cities did or did not receive power, which worried quite a few people at NASA for when the solar array was completed in the next couple of years.

The ones already built worked well. In fact, when Aldrin Base tested them just a few months before, the panels were able to power a small community of 1800 people. The only downside was that the test melted a few rovers that hadn't vacated the area in time. Clearly, there were still a few bugs that needed to be worked out.

The rover came to a stop just a few feet away from the main door to Aldrin Base. "All right, Commander, we are parked and about to disembark towards Aldrin Base."

"Be safe, team. Remember, if you see anything..."

"Don't be a hero—" the team cut her off in unison.

"We'll keep the video feed on our HUDs. Don't worry, we got this," Mike reassured her.

Harvey and the rest of the crew spent the next ten minutes sealing their EVA suits and running additional checks before finally exiting the HAB. Jessica and Harvey each grabbed a first aid kit, and Mike had a sealant gun in case anyone's suit became compromised. Once the rear capsule of the HAB depressurized, the crew entered the lunar environment.

"All right, first things first. Harvey, I need you to take a look at the generator and comms so we can see what type of damage we're dealing with," Mike said.

"On it," Harvey replied as he walked to the generator station. Each base had a main generator that was kept close by. It was enclosed enough that it was shielded from most space debris, but it was still out in the open enough to gather energy from the sun. They wouldn't know what type of situation they were walking into until Harvey was able to make sure the base had power. This main generator ran most of the base's equipment, including life-support and communications, with the other facilities. If the generator was broken, that could explain why they hadn't been able to get out any communications to Gateway or NASA. Even now, Harvey and the crew were using the HAB as a source of communication with Armstrong. The sooner he was able to fix the generator, the sooner they wouldn't have to rely on the HAB's less-than-optimal communication range. Harvey knelt next to the generator system and looked it over for only a few seconds.

"What the hell..." he began.

"Is it bad?" Jessica asked.

"No... It's...it's been switched off." Harvey flipped the switch on the generator and almost instantly, it began to power up. He checked everything over twice just to be sure, but the generator and communications array next to it all appeared to be in working order.

"What could've done that? Electrical surge? The solar storm?" the commander after listening to their exchange.

"Negative, Commander. It was literally just flipping a switch. Someone had to have turned it off."

The crew looked at the doors. Their lights were now on with the red illuminated sign hanging over the front doors saying, "WELCOME TO ALDRIN BASE."

7

The crew walked into the depressurization hatch and waited for the next few minutes while the computer system ran its checks. Normally, this would only take a few seconds, but because of the prolonged power outage, the system was extra thorough. Harvey used the terminal in the hatch to assess the rest of the base. Even with the damage from the explosion, everything looked like it was operating normally.

"Let's keep our helmets on for right now. We still aren't sure what the issues are here, so let's just be on the safe side," Mike said.

Once the doors opened, the crew walked into the large corridor. Even the hallways at Aldrin Base were bigger than those of Armstrong. To their left, the crew saw the cubbies that housed EVA suits. Most were hanging in each crew member's individual cubby, except for three empties and one suit laying on the ground. Harvey grabbed the suit, holding it up for everyone to see. The name Alana Chang was stitched into the suit, and it looked like it had been through a meatgrinder. It was torn in random spots and missing its right sleeve entirely.

"Well, I guess that explains why she was wearing Jackson's suit," Jessica said.

"Yeah, but what the hell happened to her suit in the first place?" Mike said.

"And we still don't know where Jackson and the rest of the crew are, for that matter," Harvey added, pointing at the two empty cubbies. Each cubby had its assigned astronaut's name overhead and would house each astronaut's tailor-made suit. NASA's reasoning for this was that if your suit was ill fitting, it could affect your movement and air supply—two things vitally important when moving around in outer space.

"We know Dr. Chang was wearing Jackson's suit but what about the others? Dr. Popov, Banks, and Simmons's suits are missing too. So did we miss them somewhere out there?" Jessica asked.

"I hate to say it, but if we did, they more than likely dead. Those suits only have a four-hour air supply and we found Dr. Chang almost five hours ago. We won't have any answers until you guys do a thorough sweep of the facility. Stay alert, though. We are still missing Dr. Popov, Colonel Jackson, Captain Banks, and Captain Simmons," the commander said. The crew walked silently down the corridor for a few seconds before coming up to a corner. Harvey raised his hand for the rest of the crew to stop. He then slowly looked around the corner into the next room.

"Oh my God!" he yelled as he stepped around the corner.

"What!?" Mike yelled as he ran around after him.

"Their base is so much nicer than ours!"

"For fuck's sake, Harvey! Don't do that!" Jessica snapped.

"Sorry, it's just... Look at it!"

Harvey was right, though. Where Armstrong Base had refurbished equipment from the late 2030s, Aldrin Base was equipped with every new amenity that the 2040s had to offer. Their leather chairs looked like something you'd see in an executive office. The table in the command center looked like it was a polished mahogany, despite how unrealistic that was for a lunar base. The monitors were cutting edge and the walls were shining white. They even had a state-of-the-art Kronos coffeemaker. The base was an absolute marvel to look at...until Harvey saw the command center.

The command center was almost completely destroyed. Most of the monitors were cracked and broken. The speakers were in absolute disarray, and the console itself looked like it had been hit with a sledgehammer.

"That's weird. The blast door is locked," Mike said as he made his way toward the large door behind the console. This command center was set up a bit different from the one that Harvey was used to. At Armstrong Base, the command center was the main hub of the entire base. Every single capsule connected to it. This command center looked like it was more of a greeting area than a central hub. Besides the corridor they had entered through, the only other way out of the room was through the giant blast doors that had been sealed off.

"Why do you think they locked this door but not the front? The explosion maybe?" Harvey asked.

"I'm not sure. Jessica, are you seeing anything on the air supply over there?" Mike said.

Jessica was standing by one of the few monitors that didn't have a cracked screen. From the command center, it was fairly easy to access basic information about the base, such as air supply and power output. One of the main reasons that the blast doors would be shut was if somebody put that section of the base in lockdown or if there was some sort of breach in the air supply.

"Nothing. Everything is normal according to the monitors. There shouldn't be any reason for those doors to be locked," Jessica answered.

Mike tried to open the doors using the security panel, but it was unsuccessful. "Harvey, do you think you could help me out here and hack into the security panel?"

"I mean, I can try. I'm not a hacker or anything, though. Getting into a security panel on a moon base is a little bit different than repairing one of the rovers." Harvey made his way toward Mike and used a screwdriver that he kept in his front pockets to undo the panel. He had no idea what the hell he was doing, but he thought he could at least make the effort. He stuck his screwdriver in the exposed panel as he attempted to move the wires out of place so he could get a better view of everything. He didn't want to risk hitting something important and accidentally turning off the air supply. Even though he was safe in his EVA, he didn't want to risk compromising Aldrin Base. Harvey pulled back suddenly when he felt a small shock of electricity. To everyone's surprise, the blast doors began to open.

"Fucking nailed it!" Harvey said, much louder than what he'd intended. He wasn't sure if it was because of the sudden electrical shock or the fact that he was trying to cover up that he had no idea how he'd just done that.

"Bullshit," Jessica said as she approached. The blast door was slowly opening, almost like it was caught on something.

"I knew exactly what I was doing!" Harvey retorted. After a few seconds of struggle, the large door unjammed itself and shot straight up. Jessica and Harvey stopped arguing when they saw what was on the other side. The astronauts were frozen in disbelief. The silence was finally broken when Mike spoke over the radio.

"Commander, are you guys seeing this?" he asked.

"I'm seeing it, but I'm not believing it," she replied. The corridor in front of them looked like a nightmarish version of the shining white control room they were standing in. The walls were splattered with crimson red. The floors had pools of the very same liquid scattered throughout. It looked like somebody had been dragged through these puddles, because a trail led further down the corridor and around the corner.

"Please tell me that's not—" Jessica began, but Mike cut her off.

"Blood. It's blood. Trust me on this one, guys." Mike's voice changed. In fact, his whole demeanor seemed to change. Most of the time, Mike was a laid-back guy who mostly talked about his family and laughed at fart jokes with Harvey. He was so laid-back that Harvey forgot that before he was a geologist, he was a Marine. Mike had seen combat; he had been to war. So, if Harvey was going to listen to anybody right then, it was going to be him—especially when it came to the diagnosis of large pools of blood.

"You guys stay behind me and do as I say. Is that understood?" Mike asked, his voice noticeably different, more commanding.

Neither Harvey nor Jessica said anything. They just nodded in agreement. The three of them slowly walked down the corridor, being careful not to step in the blood as they went. Mike got to a corner and took a deep breath. Harvey noticed that he was rolling his wrists, almost like he was getting ready for a fight. Mike suddenly turned the corner and immediately went into a defensive posture only to loosen up after a moment. Harvey and Jessica followed him around the corner. The two of them also ready for a fight, only to instead be met with disgust. Lying in front of them was a bloody pile of dead rats. On the floor in front of the rat pile, someone had written the word LYCAON in blood. Harvey knew that Aldrin Base had a few rats that they used for experimentation. NASA had been keeping rats on the moon for the last ten years as a long-term experiment to see the effects on their bodies. Judging by the pile in front of them, it looked like those experiments had come to an end.

"What the actual fuck…" Jessica said.

"I know this might not be the time right now, but is there any possibility that this was the reason for Dr. Chang having blood on her suit?" Harvey wondered aloud.

"Dr. Sanjay has said that the blood appeared not to be human in origin, but I'm not concerned about that right now," the commander replied.

A loud thud came from the door to the right of the group, causing them all to jump back. Unlike the door from earlier, this door was much smaller and even had a small window to peek through. There was a bright sign overhead that read, "Laboratory 2." The group stood frozen for a few seconds before they heard the thud once more, only this time they saw the source of the noise. Pressed up against the small glass panel was a human leg.

"Holy shit, there's somebody in there!" Harvey exclaimed. He took a step toward the door only to be stopped by Mike's outstretched arm. Mike said nothing; he just stared at the door and slowly walked up to it. He stopped just close enough so that he could see into the next room. He said nothing for some time before finally keying up.

"Commander, we need evacuate this mission immediately."

"I'm inclined to agree with you, Mike. Collect what you can and make sure that you look in every room on your way out. We don't want anyone getting left behind just because of a few dead bodies."

"A few dead bodies?" Harvey mouthed to Jessica in shock. The fact that the commander and Mike were so accustomed to this situation freaked him out a little bit. Mike turned away, saying nothing as he did. He only shook his head in disbelief. Harvey and Jessica approached the glass slowly, not knowing what they were about to see.

Floating in the next room were the burnt human remains of Lt Col. Jackson. The severity of the burns made it almost impossible to tell who it was, but the nametag on the burnt blue flight suit could still be read. The rest of the lab looked in utter disarray. Pieces of glass and bent animal cages floated through the room. There was also a corner of the lab that was black from what must've been the fire. If Harvey was a betting man, he would bet that this was what caused the explosion earlier. This would explain why the base was in lockdown mode until it was able to get pressurization back to normal.

"All right, team, you heard the commander. Let's finish our search for the rest of the crew, take some pictures, collect the hard drives, and get the fuck out of here," Mike commanded.

The team spent the next fifteen minutes walking through the rest of the base. They were unable to find anyone else, living or dead. Jessica found a few more writings of "Lycaon" on walls, all written in blood. After taking pictures, the group returned to the command center, where Harvey spent the next few minutes sending all pertinent data to NASA. He also copied everything onto a thumb drive before erasing the computers. No one knew how long they were going to be staying off the moon after this. NASA, like any other government agency, did not want any of their information falling into someone else's hands. Just because the United States would not return to the moon didn't mean other countries, such as Russia or China, wouldn't. Harvey put the thumb drive in his suit pocket and the three astronauts exited Aldrin Base. They made it a few feet out of the base before Mike stopped them.

"Hang on one second, guys, I want to check something." Mike walked toward the garage. The way the base was set up, the garage was connected to the Laboratory 2 capsule, which was now inaccessible. Mike walked up to the garage door and was able to open it with the security panel. Mike immediately walked in with the rest of the group following.

"Something that's been bugging me since we found Dr. Chang is the fact that she was running on the lunar surface. This base has two rovers and a HAB unit, all of which were inside for the solar storm. That means that the doctor was either unable to get to the vehicles or she was attacked when she was already outside of base." Mike shined his helmet's light on the rovers, revealing that the rover's tires were slashed, as were the HAB's.

"These tires are made of zinc and titanium woven together. The amount of force it takes to pop one of these would be astronomical," Mike said.

"What's your point?" came Greg's voice over the line.

"My point is that Dr. Chang was not able to use any of the vehicles because her path was either blocked or the vehicles themselves were damaged by something other than the lunar surface, which means..."

"Sabotage," finished the commander. The moon was already a quiet place, but this most recent revelation somehow made it quieter. Harvey had stood in graveyards that were louder. While the damage to the vehicles was extensive, it wasn't anything that he couldn't fix with the right tools and enough time. Harvey was struggling to think of any tools he had at his disposal that could do this amount of damage to the tires.

"All right, team, no more side quests. Get back to the HAB immediately. We are evacuating this mission."

"Roger that, Commander," Mike replied. The group exited the garage and closed everything back up. While they returned to the HAB, Jessica stopped suddenly and began to look around.

"Is everything okay, Jessica?" Harvey asked.

Jessica said nothing for a moment before finally turning around and continuing her walk. "I'm fine. I just feel like... I don't know. This whole situation is so creepy. I just can't help but feel like I'm being watched."

Harvey didn't say anything. He just looked around Aldrin Base to see if he could see anything strange, but the reality was that this whole thing was strange. He hoped that their visit to Aldrin Base would lead to some answers, but it had only created more questions. Questions with some seriously gruesome indications. He was finally snapped out of his thoughts when Mike told him to hurry up.

8

Harvey and the crew spent the next few minutes in silence. They gathered up whatever equipment and files they could before heading back to Armstrong. Whatever had happened at Aldrin was not an accident. Someone had deliberately disabled the security systems. What was worse was that not all of the crew was accounted for. So far, only Dr. Chang and the burnt corpse of Lt. Colonel Jackson had been found. They still couldn't find any trace of Aldrin's remaining three team members. After loading everything up, the team got into the HAB and drove away.

Mike and Jessica sat in the front of the HAB while Harvey sat in the back. The HAB was quiet, each astronaut processing everything in their own way. Someone going crazy and possibly attacking their crew was a scenario they trained for. Sure, tensions started to run a little high after a few months in space, but to kill somebody, to actually do that, it didn't make any sense to Harvey. He couldn't imagine anyone from Armstrong turning on their teammates, not even Dr. Holstrom. After what they'd seen at Aldrin Base though, it was hard to argue what had happened. Someone had deliberately messed with the equipment—perhaps even Dr. Chang was the culprit, considering how aggressive she'd been toward everyone. Whatever the reason, it looked like their four months in space was coming to an end. They were going to go back to base, get the shuttle all situated, and return home.

It wasn't all bad. He could write a book in a few years after everything became declassified, maybe even get a Lifetime movie out of it. Murder on the Moon sounded way more interesting than his planned memoir about his hatred for HOGAN.

Harvey saw the illuminated lunar surface outside of the HAB's window. It suddenly occurred to him that he was going to miss this ugly rock he'd come to call home. As barren and dangerous as it was, it was still one of the most—if not *the* most—profound experience of his entire life.

Past the lunar surface was the smallest glint of Earth off in the horizon. As he took in the beauty of his surroundings, he caught a glimpse of something on the surface that immediately caused alarm.

"STOP!" Harvey yelled.

"Fuck!" Jessica shouted as Mike slammed his foot on the brake.

"What is it? Are you hurt?" asked Mike.

Harvey wanted to tell them about the man standing outside the rover, but the only thing he managed was to raise his hand and point out the window. Standing in the distance was someone in an EVA suit. It had to be a man, Harvey thought. Jessica, Sanders, and Dr. Chang were the only women between both bases.

This man was standing, perfectly still, a couple of hundred feet away from the HAB. Mike looked out the window while Jessica crawled over him to get a better view.

"Ow, hey!" exclaimed Mike.

Jessica paid him no attention, however. Instead, she turned back around and hit the switch on the center console.

"Commander, we've found someone else from Aldrin. We are at quadrant four-twelve. They... It looks like they are just standing there..."

Harvey grabbed the binoculars from one of the rear cabinets and tried to look out the window. Jessica was right. Besides an exaggerated movement of the shoulders, the guy looked like a statue.

"Can you see who it is?" Mike asked.

"No, they're too far away. I can't even read their nametape. The suit looks rough but doesn't appear to be breached. Shit, guys, I can't tell who it is. Their sun shield is still up. I wonder if they got caught out here during the storm?"

"Commander, what should we do?" Mike asked, but before she could answer him, Jessica had hopped into the back of the rover to make her way toward the rear compartment. The rear compartment was where the crew kept their emergency EVA suits. The back door of the rear compartment was connected to a suit so that the astronauts could just crawl into the suit from the safety of the rover. Once the rover sealed itself so there was no further breach, that astronaut simply just had to eject into their suit. It prevented things like moon dust or other types of debris from getting into the rover and possibly damaging anything.

"Hey, where are you— Stop!" Mike barked.

"Look, whoever is out there is clearly running low on oxygen. You can see their shallow breathing from here. We can figure out what happened at Aldrin later. The important thing now is that we bring whoever it is out there back to base so we can have Sanjay get them checked out," Jessica countered.

"Just hold... Commander, what do you want us to do?" said Mike.

There was silence on the other end of the comms while the commander thought.

"Fine, that's fine. You can go out there, but I don't want you taking any unnecessary risks! Use extreme caution, Jessica."

"Will do, Commander," Jessica replied as she continued to get her gear on.

"Harvey, as soon as the airlock is sealed, I want you getting ready to head out so you can help," the commander ordered.

"Yes, ma'am," Harvey replied.

"He'll just slow me down, Commander. You've seen him fight," said Jessica.

Harvey wanted to argue, but the truth was that she was right.

"That may be true, but I'd feel a hell of a lot better with the two of you out there. Stay in constant communication with us and try and keep your distance until you can confirm who it is."

"Will do," Jessica answered as she closed the door to the rear airlock.

Harvey shot Mike a concerned look.

"I know, I know. Just get your gear on and be ready to help. Besides, she's probably the best choice to go out there," Mike said.

"I'm not worried about her; I'm worried about how bad things have to be for me to seem like a viable option to help her," Harvey joked.

After Jessica got herself situated in her EVA, she hit the eject button and the door shot open. The slight pressure change gave her a nice little push but not too forceful.

"Okay, I'm out and everything is in the green. I'm going to proceed with trying to make contact."

Jessica walked around to the side of the HAB. Even though Harvey and Mike could see the live feed from her helmet, they still preferred to watch from the window to get a better sense of their surroundings. Jessica walked a few feet from the HAB and waved at the figure on the horizon. If the mystery astronaut saw Jessica, he gave no indication. Besides the exaggerated breathing, they exhibited almost no signs of life.

"Okay, I guess I'll try the lights."

Jessica raised her arm and pressed a small red button on her forearm. The button created a small but very powerful red laser light to emit from her wrist. Every EVA suit was equipped with this light, and it could be seen from miles away. It was meant to be used as an alternate means of communication should anything happen to the radio equipment.

"You guys seeing anything in there?" asked Jessica.

"Nothing," Harvey replied.

"What else do we have?" she asked.

"You could try the emergency frequency? We were able to hear Dr. Chang on it earlier."

Each suit had a direct link to multiple channels that could be used to communicate with each other when out on the surface. Each team had their own set of frequencies that they could use to talk to each other without distracting the others. Most of the time, Harvey and Mike just used theirs to listen to music while they were out working—something that the commander had scolded them for on more than one occasion. Unlike the other frequencies, however, the emergency frequency was constantly monitored by each EVA suit. Mike flipped some switches in the rover so that they were now keyed up on that frequency. As soon as it was keyed up, the sound of heavy breathing permeated the HAB. Harvey and Mike gave each other a concerned look.

"Okay, we are all set in here, Jessica," Mike told her.

"Hello, can you hear me?"

The breathing stopped and the astronaut appeared to lift his head.

"This is Jessica Peoples of Armstrong Base. We are parked at your one o'clock position."

The astronaut turned his body slightly so he faced Jessica and the HAB.

"We were responding to the distress call from Aldrin Base. We have Dr. Chang safe and sound and are ready to assist you however we can..." She paused when there was no reaction. "Hello? Can you hear us?" Jessica asked, trying but failing to hide her annoyance. She turned back to look at the HAB. "Guys, I'm not getting any response. Do you want me to head back inside and we can drive over or can one of you come out to help me grab this guy?"

"I say we drive over and grab him," Harvey said.

"Yeah, he's probably dehydrated at a minimum. Alright, Jessica, new plan. We are gonna have you get back inside and we will drive ov—"

Harvey stopped listening when he saw the the horizon move. At first, he thought the man had collapsed, but when he looked through his binoculars, he realized that wasn't the case. The astronaut was now running on all-fours toward the HAB, and he was moving incredibly fast.

"Get her inside!" Harvey yelled.

"What?" Mike replied.

Harvey rushed to the front of the rover to yell into the intercom. "Jessica, get the fuck inside! He's coming right for you!"

Mike and Jessica both turned to look at the astronaut barreling toward them. The heavy breathing returned over the emergency frequency, along with what sounded like guttural growling.

"Oh fuck!" Jessica shouted as she ran toward the rear airlock. Harvey hurried to the back of the HAB to help her. Even in ideal conditions, it took a couple of minutes to get out of the EVA suit and into the airlock. Harvey looked out the window to see a small cloud of dust following the pursuing astronaut. By Harvey's best guess, he would reach them before Jessica could secure herself in the airlock. The man was moving inhumanly fast with little to no regard for the integrity of his suit.

Jessica didn't waste any time. She was already at the back of the HAB and getting herself strapped into the hatch.

"Jessica, let me know as soon as your latched and hold on tight!" Mike called back. The astronaut was getting closer. In just a few seconds, he would be at the HAB and then Jessica would be left to fend for herself without anyone to help.

"Harvey, get your helmet on," Mike ordered, who had already put his helmet back on and was managing his gloves. Harvey had already started to put his helmet on but was fumbling with the latch. The fear of not being able to get to Jessica in time caused his adrenaline to surge. The running astronaut was only ten feet away now.

"Mike, he's here! Mike, drive! Drive, Mike!" Harvey yelled. Just as he started shouting at Mike to drive, he saw the astronaut leap toward the HAB. Harvey heard another growl come over the emergency frequency, but it could have just as easily been confused for laughter.

"I'm latched!" Jessica shouted.

Without hesitation, Mike slammed his foot on gas and sped away. Or at least, the HAB's version of speeding. The airborne astronaut swiped at Jessica but missed her by mere inches. He crashed hard into the lunar surface, kicking up more debris and rock as he landed. Harvey was knocked off balance by the HAB's sudden movement but quickly readjusted himself and finished getting his EVA secured. Jessica was still hanging outside of the airlock, but she seemed secure.

"Is everyone okay?" Mike called back.

"I'm fine!" Harvey replied.

"I'm goo— Oh shit, Mike, he's chasing us again!" Jessica exclaimed.

"What do you mean? There's no way his suit isn't breached with how hard he landed."

"Look in the mirror!" she shouted.

To the crew's disbelief, she was right. Not only was the astronaut back on his feet, but he was once again on all-fours and charging toward them. Harvey looked at the mirror and saw that the astronaut's helmet was now cracked, most likely from his rough landing.

"He's breached. He's not gonna last much longer," Harvey said.

"Yeah, why don't you tell him that! Can this thing go any faster?" countered Jessica.

"Alright, everyone, calm down. We are close enough to Armstrong. I'm not about to have us swerve out of control and hurt ourselves."

Mike was right, of course. The lunar surface is dangerous at the best of times and even though the rovers they had were leaps and bounds better than the ones from the first Apollo missions, they still needed to adhere to the rough terrain on the Moon. Mike called back to Armstrong Base.

"Commander, do you read me?"

"Mike, thank God, we've been monitoring the emergency frequency."

"We are heading back to Armstrong and have our mystery guest chasing after us on foot."

"Say again?"

"We are heading back to base, but we might have some company. I need you guys to have the doors ready for us and be prepared to deal with another hostile crew member."

Jessica had made it into the airlock and was waiting for depressurization. Harvey watched her from outside, ready to pull her into the HAB as soon as the door lifted. The HAB suddenly jerked, slamming them both into the interior walls.

"Jesus, Mike, take it easy!" Harvey shouted.

"That wasn't me!" Mike looked at the side mirror and saw that not only had the astronaut caught up with them, but he was now actively trying to grab onto the back of the HAB. Harvey was helping Jessica out of the airlock when they felt another thud. Mike's gaze shifted from his side mirrors to his front windshield. He could see Armstrong Base over the horizon, but it was getting increasingly more difficult to steer. Mike was speeding, pushing the HAB to its limits. Despite that, their pursuer was keeping pace with the speeding craft.

"What keeps shaking us?" Jessica called out.

"It's him! He's hitting us!" Mike shouted back.

Mike didn't know what to think anymore; he was just in survival mode. He saw the astronaut swipe at the HAB a few more times, missing each one. Mike heard an angry roar over the emergency frequency before their attacker sped up, catching up to the HAB on their right side.

"Guys, hold on to something," Mike warned. "I think...I think he's going to T-bone us."

"He's going to what?" asked Harvey, but he quickly got his answer. The next thing Harvey felt was a hard impact from the side of the vehicle as he and the rest of the crew went airborne. He saw the HAB start to shift around him, and he reached for something, anything, to grab onto. He found a handle—for all the good it did him as the HAB and the rest of Harvey's world began to spin until it all came to a sudden stop. As the rover now lay on its side.

"Mike! Harvey! Are you there?" came the commander's just before Harvey blacked out.

9

Harvey woke up to the sound of the HAB's computer repeating the same phrase:

"*ROVER INVERTED, FLIP ROVER. ROVER INVERTED, FLIP ROVER.*" It took only a few seconds for Harvey to remember what had just happened. Some maniac running around like a dog had somehow caused the HAB to flip. Jessica was tending to Mike and trying to make sure he was okay and alert.

"Armstrong rover, come in!" came the commander's voice.

"Harvey, give me a hand here," said Jessica.

"I got you," said Harvey, who was surprisingly calm given what had just happened. Harvey crawled over to Mike, who was now alert and undoing his harness.

Jessica reached over to the console and started talking. "Commander, this is Jessica, are you reading us?"

"Jessica! Thank God. What the hell happened?"

"We're okay, or at least as okay as we can be. I think that psycho hit us," Jessica replied.

"Hit you? With what?" Sanders asked.

Mike unhooked himself from his seat and slowly dropped to the ceiling of the overturned HAB. He let out a groan before turning his attention to the console. Although he must have been in pain, Mike looked more angry than anything else. "I lost control of the HAB. That asshole was running into us, and I got distracted. I think I hit a rock or something."

"Do you still see him out there?" asked the commander.

Harvey and Jessica looked out the windows to try and see their attacker. Their view was blocked by the floating dust that surrounded the overturned vehicle. The dust cloud had completely enveloped the HAB, making it impossible to see anything.

"I can't see shit," Harvey said.

"Me either," Jessica agreed.

"Negative, ma'am. The only thing that we're seeing is a little bit of moon dust. No sign of our attacker. We will evaluate once we finish checking the integrity of our suits."

"Copy. Just try not to do anything before we get there. We are going to send a rover your way to survey the area and see what happened to your attacker."

"Understood, Commander," Mike replied.

Before the crew finished putting on their equipment, they did a quick once-over of their injuries. Mike had banged his head pretty good but was otherwise fine, Harvey's ribs were a little sore, and Jessica had landed hard on her back. All things considered, though, the three were fine. Although they could see more of the outside now, it was still riddled with dust that had been kicked up from the crash. Lunar dust could stay floating around for a while once something had stirred it up. Luckily, it looked like whoever had attacked them had left. After he finished checking his suit, Harvey crawled over to the console and pulled up the cameras. The rover had multiple cameras on its exterior that were used for both safety and documentation. Unfortunately, it looked like most of them had been damaged in the crash. He was only able to access the right-side and front cameras. Everything else just showed static. Harvey reported this to the others.

"It looks like we're only a couple hundred feet from Armstrong Base. I say that we get out and book it towards there," Jessica said.

"I don't like it," Mike said as he stared at the cameras. "We don't know if that lunatic is still out there. We could be putting ourselves in greater danger by going out there, guys. I feel much better waiting in here."

That shocked Harvey. If the Marine didn't want to fight, he knew they must really be in the shit.

"Mike, with all due respect, I don't know if we are going to have much of a choice. Look at this!" Jessica pointed to the dashboard display. The oxygen levels inside the HAB were depleting rapidly, which meant the life-support system had taken some serious damage.

"How much time?" asked Mike.

"Maybe five minutes if we're lucky," Jessica answered.

"Fuck," Mike muttered under his breath.

Harvey knew just how serious this was now. With a functioning life-support system, the crew could stay put for a few hours before they would have needed to head back to base. That would've given them and the people back at base enough time to come up with some sort of plan. At the very least, they could have waited out their attacker, who had to have next to no oxygen at this point. Now, with life support failing and their EVA suits already without a good chunk of their oxygen, time was not on their side.

"Commander, it looks like we are going to be making our way to you sooner then we would've liked. We only have a few minutes of oxygen left so we are gonna have to expedite. Keep a look out for us and have the reentry bay ready in case we have company."

"Understood, Mike. We'll be ready for you."

There was suddenly a hard thud from the back of the rover. The team looked down the narrow corridor at the airlock hatch. The bright green light labeled SECURE over the rear door shifted to a crimson red UNSECURED.

"Let's get going!" Mike said as he shifted toward the driver-side door. Mike opened the door and crawled out, followed by Jessica. As Harvey started toward the door, he began to hear scratching. He turned to see the airlock door start to shake violently. Something was trying to open it. Harvey turned to crawl out the front when he heard the door behind him rip open. his hands reached toward the outer rim of the frame, and just as he touched the surface, he felt something grip his foot. Harvey grabbed the edge of the door frame, trying to keep himself from being pulled back in. He was holding on as tight as he could, with the shitty EVA gloves being little help. It was only a matter of time before his grip would fail and he would be pulled back in with this maniac. Harvey turned to face his attacker, whose cracked visor still covered most of his face. The man was making these horrible noises as he pulled on Harvey's leg.

With his grip failing, and few options, Harvey began to kick at his attacker's face, hoping to crack his visor even more. It didn't matter how strong you were if you couldn't breathe. Harvey stomped his attacker's helmet, but this only seemed to piss him off more. His attacker's grip tightened as he started to violently pull at Harvey's leg. Pain radiated through Harvey's body as he felt his ankle pop. He felt his grip slacken when suddenly something grabbed him under his armpits and began to pull. Harvey looked up to see Jessica and Mike each pulling one of his arms. Even with their combined strength, Harvey's attacker showed no signs of letting go, but at least without having to worry about holding on for dear life, Harvey could focus more on his attacker. He started stomping a metaphorical mud hole in the man's face. With each stomp, the growls got more and more ferocious, and Harvey couldn't say if the noises were coming from him or his attacker. Eventually, Harvey felt the man's protective solar shield give way to Harvey's boot, shattering as it did. His attacker released Harvey's leg and the three astronauts landed outside the HAB. Mike was the first one to his feet, grabbing onto the door. Their attacker was back up and had already made his way to the front of the vehicle, but Mike slammed the door in his face. The attacker shot back at the rover door and attempted to hit it open. When his brute force failed, he turned to head to the back of the craft.

Jessica helped pull Harvey to his feet. He was in a lot of pain from his ankle, but his adrenaline was skyrocketing so much that he barely noticed.

"Run!" Jessica shouted as the three made for Armstrong Base.

"Fuck! He's out of the rover!" Mike yelled. "Don't look back, just keep going."

That was exactly what they all intended to do. Harvey didn't need to look back to know that this psycho was already gaining on them. He could hear the labored wheezing over the emergency channel. This guy was losing air and fast. The damage Harvey did to his face shield must have been substantial, he thought.

Jessica was a few feet ahead of the two men. She had started out in the back of the pack but was now leading it. The team could not have been more than seventy feet from Armstrong Base before something grabbed Harvey's heel and made him face-plant into the lunar surface. Harvey turned to get up, but his attacker was already on top of him.

Now Harvey got a clear look at his attacker's face. He could see he'd done more damage to the other man's helmet than he originally thought. The man's solar shield was shattered, and his face was clearly exposed, yet the attacker didn't seem to be struggling for air. The mystery attacker's suit read "Dr. Wilhelm Popov," but this man looked almost nothing like Dr. Popov. The Dr. Popov that Harvey knew was a stout man in his sixties. The only thing physically impressive about him was his beer belly. Harvey figured this man was an imposter. The crack in the attacker's visor revealed ashen pale skin and piercing yellow eyes. The man held Harvey down and slammed his head forward. Harvey moved his head to the side, but his attacker kept his head next to Harvey's neck.

What is he trying to do? Headbutt me?

The attacker shifted his head around Harvey's shoulder, growing more and more frustrated by the second.

Is he...trying to bite me?

The man on top of Harvey sat up in frustration. He raised his arms and swung. Harvey tried to move away from the blow once again, but it was no good. His attacker hit him right in the side of the head, and his ears started ringing. Worse yet, the blow created a noticeable crack in Harvey's visor. The suit wasn't going to take one more of those. As the attacker raised his other hand, Harvey heard another growl, almost as animalistic. Harvey saw his attacker look up, only to be greeted by the boots of Captain Michael Fucking Murdock as he drop-kicked the man in the face, shattering what was left of his visor.

Mike stood over Harvey, and with one hand, helped him to his feet.

"I got you, buddy," said Mike.

"Let's go. We're almost home free," Jessica, who was a few feet ahead, called.

Mike shoved Harvey toward Jessica, who was running back to help, and then turned to meet their attacker, who was already starting to get back to his feet.

"I've had a hell of a day, and I'm about done with this freaky deaky bullshit." Mike went to throw a punch at the attacker, only for it to be caught. The mystery assailant rose to his feet. He was a tower of a man, easily over six feet. Their attacker turned his head toward Mike, who seemed almost frozen in disbelief. The attacker then looked toward the others, showing his exposed face through a shattered visor.

Something about the man's crooked grin made Harvey realize that it was, in fact, Dr. Popov towering over them. That is when everyone finally saw more of his face. At first, Harvey thought maybe the doctor had been disfigured from the trauma to his helmet. But now that he was getting a better look, he realized that wasn't the case. The doctor, who once had brown eyes, now had piercing yellow eyes. His face was slightly elongated, and his nose almost had a snout-like appearance to it. The man had never been a looker, but now he looked almost alien.To the shock and horror of the crew, their attacker began to smile. He should be struggling to breathe. He should already be dead from his suit breach. Yet despite his injuries and exposure to the lunar void, he looked like he was enjoying himself.

Mike kicked the doctor in the gut. Even though Harvey never asked him, he knew that Mike had definitely killed a few people in his time. Harvey also knew that when Mike hit you, it hurt. When he kicked the doctor, though, it didn't seem to faze him. Dr. Popov swiped at Mike, sending him skipping across the lunar surface straight into a dark crater.

The Moon was a scary place, and because it had no atmosphere, any dark point, like a crater or a cavern, could be especially dangerous. Any place without sunlight means no heat. And since the Moon had no atmosphere and couldn't retain heat, these dark spots could get into the negative hundreds of degrees. The fact that Harvey and Jessica couldn't see Mike meant that he was knocked into one of those icy death traps. The astronaut's EVA suits could regulate the extreme temperatures to a degree, but if Mike's suit had been breached, he had only a couple of minutes before he froze to death.

Jessica and Harvey ran toward the doctor. Without speaking, both seemed to have the same idea that he couldn't overpower two of them. The next thing Harvey knew, he and Jessica were knocked back a few feet onto their asses.

They got back to their feet. Jessica went high and Harvey went low. Harvey's plan was to tackle the doctor, but that very clearly wasn't going to work. The doctor didn't even budge when Harvey drove his shoulder into him. Jessica grabbed Popov's arm, only for him to pull her close. With a breached suit, they could no longer hear the horrible noises the doctor was making, which they were perfectly fine with given that the doctor's mouth shifted more and more into a canine-like snout. Harvey couldn't tell if the doctor was laughing, growling, or yelling, but whatever it was, he knew it was bad. Dr. Popov went to bite at Jessica, but she was able to jam her fingers into his exposed eyes, making him stumble back and yell in pain.

"Get up," she said. "Let's get Mike and get out of here."

As they ran over to the crater that Mike had been knocked into, a hand rose from the darkness like a creature from a Romero movie. Mike looked rough, but he was alive. They grabbed a hold of him and pulled him out of the pit, only for him to look at them and yell, "Watch out!"

Both astronauts turned and saw Dr. Popov charging them. He would have tackled all three into the pit had Mike not pushed Harvey and Jessica away. As the doctor lunged, Mike squatted down and let the charging man's momentum do the rest of the work. He pushed up from under his attacker and flipped the doctor into the pit. Dr. Popov floated helplessly for a few seconds before disappearing into the darkness. All three astronauts stared into the pit. Mike was the first one to speak.

"With exposure like that, no way he survives more than a few seconds down there. Let's get back to base and get stitched up."

Harvey and Jessica moved to either side of Mike and helped him walk, but as they turned toward Armstrong, Mike gasped. His body suddenly jolted up, and Jessica and Harvey turned to see Mike being ripped away from them. Dr. Popov had driven his hand straight through Mike's abdomen and out the other side. Mike let out a horrible scream, and the doctor flung him to the ground, shaking his hand free. Blood floated off the doctor's hand as he started to march toward the other two. Both astronauts were frozen in fear, but somehow, some way, Mike was able to grab the doctor's leg.

"Run," Mike yelled. "Run, now. I can't hold him for long."

Dr. Popov, who seemed somewhat amused by the Marine trying to grapple with him, lifted Mike into the air.

Harvey tried to reach out for his friend, but Jessica had already grabbed his outstretched hand and was pulling him away.

"Come on, Harvey! Do what he says," Jessica urged.

It took every ounce of control for Harvey not to turn and help Mike as he screamed in pain. Harvey turned and started running. The screams eventually stopped, but the silence was somehow worse.

As they got closer to Armstrong Base, the doors opened. Commander Sanders and Sanjay were waiting for them, waving frantically.

"Run!" they kept yelling. "Run as fast as you can!" Harvey turned to see Dr. Popov chasing them on all-fours again. When they got within ten feet of the hatch, Jessica and Harvey both leapt in as Sanders hit the emergency lockdown button. The hatch doors shut just in the nick of time, and there was a loud thud as Dr. Popov rammed into it. There was still a small window on the door for everyone to look out. The doctor pressed his face against the glass, growling and banging his fist into the panels. The doors were made to survive meteor strikes, but even so, the doctor was hitting it with enough force that it began to dent. Sanders stared at him, and Harvey couldn't tell whose gaze was more intimidating. Dr. Popov appeared to calm down somewhat as he looked around the door frame. He focused on the outside access panel and started to press at it. His deformed hand was trembling as he attempted to carefully press buttons. It looked like he was doing his best to focus but each try only generated an incorrect chime.

"It's no use! We are on lockdown. It doesn't matter what you do, you're not getting in here without the code, dipshit," the commander said. This clearly angered Dr. Popov, who started to bang his head against the door.

Eventually, the doctor stopped and brought his face up to the glass once more, but this time, he wasn't staring at them. He was sniffing. He sniffed so aggressively it was almost like he was trying to inhale their scent. His eyes darted around the room, going back and forth between everyone before fixing his gaze on the commander. A wicked grin appeared across his elongated mouth. Suddenly, Dr. Popov dropped back to all-fours and ran off across the barren lunar surface.

10

"Fuck!" Harvey shouted as Sanjay dropped him roughly onto a table in the medical bay.

"Sorry! I'm sorry. I need to take your suit off you but before I do, I need you to tell me where it hurts," Sanjay said.

"My leg... Fuck, everywhere, just numb me up!"

Now that the adrenaline had worn off, Harvey was becoming all too aware of his injuries. His forearm throbbed, and his left leg hurt more than anything he had ever experienced. He knew it was bleeding because of the pool of blood that had formed at his heel and soaked through his white boot. He wasn't sure if these injuries were a result of the HAB crash or Dr. Popov. The only thing that he knew for sure was that he was in a lot of pain. The commander and Jessica came in behind them. Jessica had already removed the top portion of her EVA suit. She was covered in bruises all along her arms and back. Her lip was bleeding, and she had the start of a black eye. Despite all that, she was still standing.

"Just run through it with me," Sanders said.

"Samantha, you know as much as we do. I don't know what the fuck that thing is, but you saw what it did. It...it got Mike." Jessica was trying to hold back tears. "It got him and there wasn't jack shit that we could do about it. Whoever or whatever that thing is, it was moving around with a breached suit. A breached suit in fucking outer space!" Jessica punched the wall next to her.

Sanders pulled Jessica in for a hug. Jessica seemed to resist her at first but eventually began to sob in the commander's embrace.

"That thing is Dr. Popov. I saw his—shit, Sanjay!—I saw his nametag when he had me on the ground," Harvey said as Sanjay tried to remove his suit.

"Commander, please report to the command center," Greg said over the PA. Sanders was in no mood to respond to his every beck and call, but he elaborated before she could ask him to. "It's... It's that thing. It's coming back. It's coming back to the airlock. It looks like it has something..."

Without a word, Jessica turned and ran for the airlock. Harvey started to sit up before the commander pushed him back down.

"No! You two stay. Jessica and I will see what's going on." She pointed at the two men and mouthed the word "stay" before running after Jessica.

Within a matter of seconds, the two had made it back to the airlock door located in the garage. The door's glass panel was big enough that both women could see the doctor moving outside. He was walking toward the door. His walk had changed to a trudge as he made his way toward the door, clearly dragging something with him. The darkness outside made it difficult to see what he was carrying until he got closer.

"Oh my god!" Jessica whispered as the creature slammed Mike's dead body into the glass. Half of his face had been slashed off. The part that remained was covered in frost and had an expression of horror. Mike's last moments of excruciating pain, forever frozen in place.

Harvey and Sanjay entered the command center only to see Greg glued to the monitors. Sanjay had finished removing Harvey's torn suit and had given him a crutch. Harvey instantly recognized who the creature was holding. He limped over to the monitor as fast as he could, pushing Greg and Sanjay out of the way. If the two men said anything in protest, he didn't hear. He was too fixated on the screen. He gripped the edges of the monitor as hard as he could. He didn't do this out of anger, although he was certainly feeling that. Instead, he held on to the monitor to steady himself as shook uncontrollably.

"Oh God, no..." he said, his voice a little above a whisper before his emotions took over. "No, no, no, no, no! You fucking son of a bitch, put him down!" Harvey screamed as tears began to roll down his face.

Jessica winced as she turned away from the door. The creature began rubbing Mike's corpse along the glass. He was gentle at first, but only for a short time. The monster then began to press Mike's corpse into the door so hard it caused what remained of his helmet to shatter.

Where Jessica had looked away, Commander Sanders had stayed fixated on the monster. She refused to show any fear, even though her heart felt like it was about to beat out of her chest. Dr. Popov started to bang Mike's skull against the door, ruining what was left of his face. The enraged creature continued for several seconds before he'd finally had enough. He gripped what remained of Mike's body between his massive hands and began to pull until the frozen carcass ripped in two. The creature unceremoniously threw Mike's lower half onto the ground while using his top half to hit the door one last time, denting it in the process. Dr. Popov looked through the glass, and that was when the two women were able to get a clear look at him. Beyond the elongated muzzle they'd seen before, the exposed skin was ashen gray with patches of dark hair. His ears had now grown and become pointed at the top. The most disturbing part, however, were his eyes. The yellow eyes now glowed as they looked in from the darkness. They were predator eyes, and they were fixated on the women inside. Dr. Popov was no more. Now there was only a monster. The doctor sniffed at the door before turning his head toward the sky and howling.

Commander Sanders said nothing. She clenched her fists and stared through teary eyes.

"It's a goddamn werewolf!" Harvey shouted as the other men stared blankly at the monitor, unsure of what they were seeing. The wolf howled for what seemed like minutes before he finally lowered his body and ran away.

"No, no, it's not a werewolf. They are clearly suffering from some sort of—"

"Oh, for fuck's sake, Greg! He has ears, a snout, and he just ran away on all-fours after howling at the moon...*while he is on the fucking moon!*"

Before Greg could respond, a scream came from the medical bay. Before anyone could ask what it was, Sanjay already knew.

"Dr. Chang..." he said softly before running off. Harvey chased after him, as best he could on his injured leg, with neither man saying anything.

"Wha...he...hey! Wait!" Greg yelled, but neither of the men stopped.

Greg's voice came over the PA system again.

"Commander, could you please make your way back to medical? There appears to be a situation with Dr. Chang."

Without a word between them, Jessica and Sanders started sprinting back to the medical bay. The commander only hoped that she would not have to knock out the doctor again.

Sanjay was already tending to Dr. Chang when Harvey limped in behind him. Dr. Chang was screaming, thrashing against her restraints.

"What do you need me to do?" Harvey asked.

Sanjay was looking at the vital signs monitor in disbelief before he turned to rummage through drawers. Between Chang's screams, the alarms, and Sanjay yanking the drawers and cabinets open, the room was utter chaos.

"Uh, just, um, try and keep her calm," said a panicked Sanjay. Harvey limped over to Chang without a clue about how to calm her down. The woman was alternating between incoherent screams and guttural growls.

"Uh, Alana... It's Harvey...the guy you punched..."

Harvey had no idea what to say to this woman, but luckily, he didn't have to.

"Yes!" Sanjay exclaimed as he turned, syringe in hand. Without hesitation, he plunged the syringe into Chang's IV tube, and in a few seconds, she started to calm down. Her breathing slowed and she stopped screaming. Her eyes started to close and to the surprise of everyone, she started to speak.

"Harvey..." she whispered.

"Yes, Alana, I'm here. Are you okay?" he asked.

"They're going to kill you..." she said in a low tone.

The words cut into Harvey, but before he could react, Dr. Chang started to laugh. That was when Harvey noticed her teeth and how pointed they had become. She opened her eyes, revealing a dark yellow glow. In one swift motion, she broke her right arm free of its restraints. The men had never seen someone move so fast as she grabbed Sanjay by the throat.

"They're going to kill you all," she said with a smile. Harvey was no longer thinking about the situation. He only knew that he needed to free Sanjay. Without a second thought, he raised his crutch and swung it at Chang's head as hard as he could. It was a clean shot but judging by the doctor's face, it did little more than annoy her. She threw Sanjay at Harvey, sending both men flying into the corridor. Even in 1/6 of Earth's gravity, the impact was enough to knock the wind out of them both.

Harvey was horrified to see that Dr. Chang was now free of her restraints and laughing as she towered over the two men. At first, he thought it was his eyes playing tricks on him, but when she took a step forward, there was no mistaking it. The once 5'5 doctor now stood over six feet tall. Harvey noticed that her nails had already started to grow to a point. She crouched through the doorway and raised her arm, ready to bring it down in one powerful swipe. Harvey closed his eyes and waited for the impact. Instead, the next thing he heard was a scream that quickly turned into a yelp. He felt someone tug at his collar and opened his eyes to see Jessica.

"Get up! We gotta move!" she yelled. Jessica pulled Harvey and a disoriented Sanjay to their feet, pulling both with her. Harvey also felt someone pushing at his back. He turned and saw Sanders behind him. His gaze was then pulled to Dr. Chang, who had one hand over a bloody eye while she swiped violently at the air with the other. Harvey wasn't sure, but he thought he saw something sticking out of her eye.

"You bitch! Fucking cunt!" Chang screamed.

Jessica was pulling so hard at the two men that all three fell as they tumbled through the entrance to the command center. Commander Sanders followed them in and stood in the doorway.

"Now, Greg! Shut it!" she commanded.

Without missing a beat, Greg entered the lockdown command on the console. The door sealed shut, initiating a full lockdown of the command center. The astronauts heard a loud bang as Dr. Chang slammed herself into the newly-sealed door.

"Pull her up on the monitor," Sanders said as she began flipping switches on the command console. Chang appeared on the main monitor. She was growling as she swung her arms wildly at the door. When that didn't work, she started to claw at other parts of the corridor. She continued until she heard the commander's voice over the PA.

"Alana, I have some questions, and you're going to answer them. If you do not cooperate, I am going to jettison the whole medical capsule with you in it. Is that understood?"

Dr. Chang said nothing. She ripped the pen out of her eye.

"Good, let's start with a basic one. What happened at Aldrin Base?"

Chang's smile returned, but she said nothing.

"Let's try this again. What happened..."

"Do you really think your empty threats have any sway over me, Samantha? I know exactly where I'm standing. You won't jettison this capsule. If you do, you'll risk compromising the life support system. No, I think I'm just peachy and this door won't hold me back for long."

"Alana, I am not making empty threats, now please..."

Dr. Chang cut her off once more. "Mike's dead, isn't he?"

Sanders said nothing.

"Yes, yes, yes, I could smell it. It was all over that little bitch Harvey. Who got him? Simmons? Banks? Oh, was it Dr. Popov? I bet they ripped him apart. Tell me, did you see the base? Did you see what they did? How is Lt Col Jackson?"

The doctor turned her head to look directly at the camera. "Did you see Lycaon?"

Commander Sanders, to her credit, continued to show no reaction to Chang's questions. "What happened to you?" she asked instead.

This question seemed to have some effect on Dr. Chang. Although her smile remained, the woman was now clearly sobbing.

"It's already too late. There's no stopping them." She started to hyperventilate as she turned back to the command center door. "There's no stopping us!" She slammed her head into the door. She started to scream and tried to claw her way in. Sanders tried to get her to respond again, but it was no use. Dr. Chang was possessed in her attempt to break through the door.

"Do it," Sanders said coldly.

"Commander, I think that the integrity of the door will hold. It's not worth compromising the—"

"If she keeps going at this rate, it's only a matter of time until she gets in. I'm not asking you. I'm telling you. Jettison the capsule."

"Commander, I—"

"You're useless," the commander stated as she pushed Greg away from the control panel. She started typing in the jettison command but didn't initiate it. She looked up at the monitor—specifically looked up at Dr. Chang and studied her. She wondered how such a resilient person could turn into such a monster. She keyed up the PA once more.

"Alana... I'm sorry."

Commander Sanders hit the initiate command and the facility started to shake. The crew briefly heard what sounded like latches shifting, followed by a loud grinding and then...nothing. On the monitor, the astronauts saw Dr. Chang continuing her assault on the door, despite the clear shaking around her. As the capsule started to disengage and the air seal was broken, the camera showed Chang thrown around before the camera feed cut out and was replaced by static.

11

Alarms were blaring throughout Armstrong Base. Most of the crew had lost their footing when Commander Sanders ejected Dr. Chang —or more accurately, Dr. Chang and the entire eastern portion of Armstrong Base. Under ideal conditions, jettisoning a portion of the base should be done after a thorough check of the base's integrity and all life-support systems, as well as all resources moved to other sections. These circumstances, of course, were less than ideal.

"Someone, turn off that alarm! Greg, I need you to find me a feed of the jettisoned capsule," Sanders ordered.

"Commander, the life-support systems are at sixty percent, which is twenty percent from what we need to be able to survive another solar storm. Plus, there is the issue of us no longer having a medical facility or more importantly, my lab!" retorted Dr. Holstrom.

"Damn it, Greg, find the capsule! We need to make sure she is dead."

Dr. Holstrom furiously typed into the command console. In a few seconds, he pulled up the camera controls around Armstrong Base and began to cycle through their feeds. Meanwhile, Harvey struggled to get to his feet. He used a computer desk to help steady himself before sitting and turning off the alarm system. The rest of the team was anxiously looking at the large screen in the center of the room.

"Wait, that was it, go back two!"

Dr. Holstrom cycled back to the requested feed, and what appeared on the big screen left the whole crew speechless. What remained of the east wing of Armstrong Base was now a crumbled heap of plastic spread over the lunar surface. The debris of what used to be valuable medical equipment, supplies, and personal belongings was now a frozen mess.

"Commander, there's no way she could've survived that," Sanjay said.

"The other one doesn't seem to have any issues out there," Jessica pointed out.

Commander Sanders said nothing. She stared at the screen, waiting for some sign of life from the wreckage. Quiet minutes passed before the commander's suspicions were confirmed.

"No fucking way..." Harvey whispered

Dr. Alana Chang was battered and broken, but she was alive. The doctor's left arm was hanging by a shred of skin. Her good arm, if you could call it that, had multiple pieces of jagged bone sticking out of it. Despite that, she was using it to crawl out of the jettisoned capsule. Even in the vacuum of space, it was obvious she was screaming with every movement. Once she was all the way out of the wreckage, the crew was able to see the mangled mess of what used to be her legs.

"She shouldn't... She should be dead. This isn't possible," Dr. Holstrom said in disbelief.

"Whether it's possible or not, it's happening," Jessica said flatly.

The group's focus shifted when alarms started blaring again.

"Harvey, I thought you turned those off?" asked the commander.

"I turned off the life-support alarms. These are the security alarms."

"Meaning what?" Jessica asked.

Harvey entered some commands on the keyboard and pulled up the security cameras around the perimeter of the base.

"Meaning we have company." Harvey moved away from his monitor to show the rest of the crew. There were three areas that had picked up movement. Each camera showed a shadowy figure running past it, each a different size. The only one that was clear was Dr.

Popov, who was much more wolf than man at this point. He lumbered past the camera, his gaze fixated on the wreckage.

"Look!" Dr. Holstrom shouted as he pointed up at the main screen. The main screen still showed Dr. Chang miserably crawling away from the wreckage but now she had an audience. A shadowy figure with yellow eyes walked on all fours towards Chang but stopped just a few feet away from her. The man, if you could call him that, wore a torn blue jumpsuit that was usually worn underneath an EVA. He was gray in complexion and covered in fur just like Dr. Popov, however he lacked the doctor's impressive size. A second figure came into view from the opposite side. This figure was similar in stature and appearance to the first, blue jumpsuit and all. He also got relatively close to Dr. Chang, who was just now realizing that she was no longer alone. The two figures stood over Chang, studying her, looking like they were ready to attack at any moment.

"I'm guessing that's Simmons and Banks," Sanders said.

"What are they doing?" asked Sanjay.

"Waiting."

"Waiting for what?" Holstrom asked.

"Him," Harvey answered.

Dr. Popov's impressive frame came into view on the screen. He stared at Dr. Chang but didn't do anything. Chang looked like she was trying to talk to him.

"How could she hope to communicate with them? They are in a vacuum! That means no sound," complained Dr. Holstrom.

"Dr. Chang woke up right when Dr. Popov started howling. Maybe there is some sort of special frequency or telepathy they can use," Sanjay said.

"Like Professor Xavier or Martian Manhunter or—" Harvey started to contribute before Dr. Holstrom cut him off.

"This isn't some comic book fantasy! This is real life, dammit!"

"Greg, there are literal werewolves on the moon. I'd say that real life has gone out the fucking window," Jessica snapped.

It looked like Dr. Chang was going back and forth between talking and barking at Dr. Popov and the rest of the pack. While the crew had no idea what she was saying, one thing was certain: she looked scared.

Dr. Popov didn't seem interested in whatever she had to say. Although he stood over her at first, he'd begun circling her when she began to talk. He looked much more interested in the wreckage than her, but he turned suddenly when Chang yelled at him. This put his full attention on her now. Popov knelt so that he was eye level with Chang, who was now visibly weeping. He reached out with his giant arm and brought his claws to her face. Chang winced away, clearly expecting him to slash at her, but he didn't do that. Instead, he gently caressed her disfigured face. This continued for a few seconds before Popov suddenly stopped and brought his other claw up to her face. He held Dr. Chang like that for a few minutes before he started to move his mouth at her.

Whether he was talking or not, the crew had no idea. Truthfully, they weren't paying attention to that as they were all too focused on Popov's hands. More specifically, they focused on his giant thumbs that he slowly pushed toward Chang's eyes. Knowing what was coming, Dr. Chang tried to shake free, but it was no use. Popov slowly pressed his thumbs into her eyes. If it wasn't for the silence of space, her scream would have been deafening. Popov held his grip for a few seconds before violently releasing her. He barked at the other two that had been waiting their turn. The wolves that were once Simmons and Banks wasted no time as they lunged at Chang's writhing body. Popov stood and stared at the camera. He started to lick Chang's blood off his claws. His eyes rolling back as he did so, clearly enjoying the carnage a little too much. He smiled up at the camera and mouthed something before turning his attention back to the feeding frenzy.

As the wolves fed, something about them seemed to change. It was hard to tell at first but as the feeding continued, the monsters appeared to be getting bigger. Simmons and Banks started to grow to the point that they were almost ripping out of their jumpsuits. Despite the increase, neither wolf came close to matching Dr. Popov's size. As his pack began to grow, so did the good doctor. Dr. Popov now looked to be almost as large as the LTV rovers.

The crew was quiet at this point. Every time they thought things couldn't get worse, they somehow did. Harvey was trying to think of something to say to pull everyone back from the camera feed, but Dr. Holstrom beat him to it, summarizing what was going through everyone's mind.

"We are all going to die up here."

12

The crew hadn't left the command center. The pack had finished their feeding frenzy a couple of hours ago. They'd picked her clean, leaving nothing but bones. Chang was unfortunately alive for most of it. This led Sanjay to hypothesize that they must have possessed some sort of healing factor but without an actual study, it was just a hypothesis.

The pack remained even after they'd finished with Chang. Harvey knew that you didn't have to be an animal expert to know what they were doing. Whether they were looking for weak spots or just waiting for something else to happen, the pack had chosen their next meal. Harvey and the rest of the crew knew it was only a matter of time until they had to come face to face with their fate.

The crew had spent the last couple of hours getting an assessment of Armstrong's life-support system. After checking that and getting a count of resources, the prognosis wasn't good. Life support had been heavily damaged during the emergency jettison of Dr. Chang and the east wing. Harvey did what he could, but the most crucial parts of the system weren't salvageable. By his estimates, they would run out of air in the next three months—so long as there wasn't another solar storm or meteor shower. The other issue they faced was food. The cafeteria and most of the crew's food had been in the eastern wing. After Sanjay and Jessica took count, they estimated that the base now had enough food to sparingly feed four people for the next two weeks. Whether they faced the pack or starvation, the crew's outlook wasn't good.

After getting all the information, Commander Sanders contacted Vince Notley and Lt Col. Hannon for a conference call. As always, Vince didn't mince words

"For Christ's sake, Samantha, I have been trying to reach you for the last few hours. What the fuck is going on up there?"

If the commander was fazed, she didn't show it. She was all business at this point.

"Gentlemen, last we spoke, the crew was confronting a hostile member of Aldrin Base. It is my duty and my regret to inform you that Captain Michael Murdock was killed by that crew member. We have good reason to believe it was Dr. Popov."

"Hold on, just wait a minute, you're telling me that Mike was—"

"That isn't all," Sanders interrupted. "Believe me, gentlemen, that is the least-ridiculous thing I have to report. Astronauts Howlett and Peoples were able to return to Armstrong Base while Captain Murdock attempted to stall Dr. Popov. It needs to be noted that he died valiantly and in service to his crew and the mission."

That last sentence led to Commander Sanders shedding a tear. It was clear that she was doing her best to hold it together.

"What I have to tell you next is going to seem impossible in every sense of the word, which is why I asked Astronaut Howlett to send you the video files that have been collected over the last few hours. That email was sent a half hour ago. I have no doubt that some of the techs have already analyzed it and have given you a raw report, Vince. Rest assured that the footage is real. I am going to try and fill you in as best I can."

A NASA technician handed Vince a packet of papers that Harvey guessed had pictures of the werewolves in them. Vince skimmed through the packet as his expression changed from confusion to alarm. Vince kept his gaze on the photos when he started to speak.

"You have my undivided attention, Samantha..."

"We believe that the crew of Aldrin Base was exposed to something and while we don't know the origins, the effects are undeniable."

Judging by the background noise, Lieutenant Colonel Hannon was watching one of the videos of Dr. Chang after she started to change.

"What the hell is this?" whispered the colonel, but Sanders kept on with her story.

"By now you have both watched the videos, so I am just going to cut to the chase. We believe that the crew of the Aldrin have somehow changed into something akin to werewolves."

"Samantha..." Vince started in a disbelieving tone.

"We don't have all of the information right now, but I'd say that's a pretty damn accurate description at the moment. As far as we can tell, Dr. Chang was already infected when we found her wandering around. By the time she got to the station, she was already starting to feel the effects. When Dr. Popov attacked Armstrong Base, it...accelerated Chang's change. It took the efforts of almost everyone on board just to lock her into the east wing."

"Samantha... Our records are showing that the east wing of Armstrong has been jettisoned..."

"We had no choice, Vince. Dr. Chang was changing into one of those things at an alarming rate. She seemed to be getting stronger by the minute. If we didn't jettison the capsule, then..."

"Oh, that's horseshit, Samantha!" interrupted Dr. Holstrom. Up until this point, the rest of the crew had kept quiet like Commander Sanders had requested. Dr. Holstrom clearly saw this conference call as a way to air his grievances. He marched over to the commander and pointed his finger within inches of her face.

"We have no proof that Dr. Chang would have gotten through that door. You made a rash decision and now, because of your impulsiveness, we are more likely to die from the life support failing or starvation than we are being attacked by those...things! This would have never happened if you would have kept me as the mission lead. I want the record to show that I was the only one adamantly against jettisoning the capsule."

Commander Sanders never broke eye contact with Dr. Holstrom.

Any trace of emotion on her face from speaking about Mike or Dr. Chang had disappeared.

"Greg, I'm sure that you are very tense, just like the rest of the crew. I will be more than happy to answer to an investigative panel whenever we get back to Earth. I stand by my decision, though, and make no mistake, the reason that I am in charge and not you is because I actually have to balls to make those decisions. Now get your goddamn finger out of my face."

The commander didn't need to tell Holstrom what would happen if he didn't listen. Her face told him everything he needed to know. Dr. Holstrom very wisely lowered his finger, but he still stared her down as some form of defiance.

"As I was saying, we had no choice but to jettison the capsule. Now for the bad news."

This gave Vince a sick chuckle.

"That wasn't the bad news?" Hannon asked.

"Not all of it. After looking over everything with the team, we have concluded that our life-support system is on its last legs, and we only have enough food to last us for two weeks at the most."

"What if you ration your supplies?" Hannon asked.

"That is with rationing our supplies."

"Look, I'm not trying to talk down to you, but maybe you guys miscalculated. Why don't you send us the numbers and let our teams here give everything a look. Maybe we can find something to—"

"Vince, we have run the numbers. Over and over again. Check our email that we sent earlier. I'm sure your teams will confirm what we already know. It's one of the main reasons we waited so long to call you guys. We needed to be sure so that we could lay out all our cards on the table. We have three months before the life support gives out and two weeks before we start to starve to death."

"What about the other supply crates? Surely those would help. Did you think of those?" Vince asked.

"We did, and they would be very helpful, but we lost direct access to that portion of the base when we jettisoned Alana. If we want to get to those supplies, we would need to get in an EVA suit and pray that those things out there don't catch us. Truth be told, I've seen what they did to Mike and Alana. I'd rather starve."

Vince said nothing, but he did nod in agreement. The man now had his massive arms crossed and was no longer looking at the screen. He was very clearly lost in thought.

"Okay, so food and resources aren't an option. Maybe we can land one of the Gateway shuttles," Hannon offered.

"We appreciate the offer, Phil, but that still won't do us much good with those things out there. There is no way they wouldn't notice you guys landing and even if we distract them somehow, there's no way we could do it long enough for everyone to get safely aboard the shuttle and initiate a launch."

"What about the Collins Communication Array? Could you get to that?" Vince asked, his voice perking up slightly.

"We thought of that too, but just one of those things was fast enough to catch up to our HAB. When he—Dr. Popov—did catch them, he was able to flip the HAB. He's only gotten bigger since that attack earlier. Even if Harvey disables the governor on the LTVs, there's no telling if we'd make it. And before anyone suggests waiting these things out, we have been seeing them for the last five hours. All three of them are clearly exposed to the effects of space and they don't seem to mind it in the least. I don't think this is a wait-and-see scenario..."

"It sounds like you have certainly thought of everything, Samantha..." Vince was now looking sullenly at the monitor. He looked at someone off-screen and gave a slight nod.

"Phill... Samantha... I am going to need to call you guys back. Please know that we are going to do everything we can to get you all home safe. No matter what, I am bringing you guys home. I'll call you back momentarily."

The main screen went black, but Harvey could no longer contain himself.

Harvey needed to get out of the room. He felt like he was suffocating, hell, who was he kidding, life support was failing. He was suffocating! "Fuck this! Where is the goddamn Space Force when you need them!" he yelled.

He walked out of the command center and to the only place that he truly ever felt at peace: the garage. Once he got down there, he went over to his desk. He meant to sit, but this was the first time since getting back to base where there wasn't something he was supposed to be doing. Finally, the gravity of everything got to Harvey and he broke down. He grabbed a tool from his desk and threw it at the ground as hard as he could. He couldn't even see what he had thrown due to the tears in his eyes. He then proceeded to bang his fists on the workbench before sliding to the ground. He just sat there for a while and let everything from the last few hours wash over him.

At some point during his breakdown, he felt Jessica walk in. She said nothing but wrapped her arms around him and held him tight. They stayed like this for a while before Jessica finally spoke.

"Have you eaten anything yet today, shithead?"

It was subtle, but for some reason, it was exactly what he needed to hear to perk him up. Harvey started to laugh and wiped the tears from his eyes.

"No... Honestly, I haven't even been hungry since the breakfast debacle earlier. I planned on eating when we all watched the game later. That reminds me..."

Harvey stood and went to the computer on his workbench and began clicking.

"Ha, son of a bitch..."

Harvey saw the scores on the computer. OSU beat Michigan, 10-3.

"Could you imagine how much shit he would be talking right now?"

"I'm sure he had something good planned if Michigan won," Jessica said.

"Oh, I can't even imagine. That jarhead was downright diabolical with his pranks."

"I guess now is as good a time to tell you as any. We had this great plan to scare you a few weeks ago using HOGAN."

"Jessica, at this point, I don't know if anything will ever be as scary as what's going on right now."

"Yeah, yeah, I get that, but you'll like this one. The plan was that we were going to have HOGAN waiting for you in your room and when you went to bed, he would grab you. We had this whole thing planned out where he was going to seem like he had come to life and was breaking the rules of robotics and everything, but we ended up breaking him, so instead we..."

Harvey stopped listening to Jessica at that point as a wave of clarity washed over him. He stood and looked at Jessica, who couldn't tell if he was angry or not about the prank.

"Hey, come on, I thought we were in a safe space here..."

Harvey grabbed Jessica's face and kissed her on the forehead. "You're a demented genius!" he exclaimed before he proceeded to limp back toward the command center. When he ran in, with Jessica close at his heels, the team was in deep discussion with Vince and Hannon again. Harvey needed to get everyone's attention somehow, so he said the first thing that popped into his head.

"Hey, everybody, shut up!"

It wasn't subtle, but it worked.

"Harvey, what the hell—" Sanders began before Harvey cut her off. Under normal circumstances, he would be terrified of the woman, but he had more important things on his mind.

"Sorry, but look, I...I have a plan to get us out of here...but you're not going to like it."

13

The crew spent the next couple of hours in the garage loading up essential supplies and gear into the two remaining LTVs. Unlike the HAB, these rovers were much smaller and didn't have any life-support systems on board. This meant that its passengers were completely exposed to the elements. Harvey was finishing getting fastened into Rover Two while the rest of the group finished loading up Rover One. After getting settled in, Harvey started to look himself over one more time, ensuring he could move okay in his new suit.

"How're you looking over there, Harv?" the commander asked.

"Everything is checking out okay right now. How about you guys? You almost done fucking around over there?"

"We are good to go here, just need to get settled in," Sanjay replied.

Sanjay moved into the rear passenger seat behind Jessica. Holstrom was sitting in the front passenger seat while Jessica was finishing her inspection of the rover from the driver's seat. Commander Sanders walked up behind Harvey and patted the top of his helmet.

"How're you feeling in there? Any second thoughts?" Sanders asked, her voice a little above a whisper.

"No, no second thoughts, ma'am. I'm feeling pretty good about this plan."

"Ha, well, that at least makes one of us. I know I've already said it countless times already, but most people would think this plan of yours is suicide. Hell, Vince even called it the craziest idea NASA has ever heard."

"Then why let us do it?" asked Harvey.

"Because, lucky for you, I like crazy. Don't get us killed, kid." Commander Sanders lightly punched Harvey's arm and then walked to Rover One.

"Alright, team, I know we have briefed this to death, but we are going to go over this one more time. As soon as those doors go up, Harvey is going to drive out of here like a bat out of hell. We will wait a few seconds to see if the pack takes the bait and then we will be on our way to the shuttle. We will launch and rendezvous with Gateway, and Harvey... Well, Harvey knows what he has to do. If for some reason they don't take the bait and we are exposed out there, the plan is to drive to Collins and wait for further instructions from NASA. They have enough supplies to last us for the next couple of years. Does anyone have any questions?"

"I would like to state for the record that I am vehemently against this plan," Holstrom said.

"So is NASA, Greg, but you aren't the one being used for bait. Anyone else?"

"Harvey, are you sure that the governor has been disabled?" Jessica asked.

"I'm positive, Jess. You guys should have no problem hitting sixty if you need to. Just don't be a typical woman driver and you should be fine," Harvey said with a smirk.

Jessica said nothing, just flipped Harvey off. Teasing Jessica was the only thing Harvey could do to keep his mind off the situation. It helped him feel a sense of normality, but the fact he was missing Mike was all too prevalent still in his head. Commander Sanders fastened herself in the seat next to Sanjay and gave Harvey a thumbs-up.

"Alright, Harvey, it's your show now," came the commander's voice in his helmet.

"Yes, ma'am!" Harvey held up the garage door opener to show the crew. "I am going as soon as I hit this button. You guys wait for me to tell you when I get them all to follow and then get the hell out of here. Good luck, guys."

Harvey pressed the device and then gripped the steering wheel with both hands. He was gripping so hard, he thought he might break it. The lights on the garage door changed from green to red, indicating that the garage was starting to depressurize. The air breach alarms started to sound throughout the base but disappeared as soon as the garage doors started to open. Harvey was already sweating and had to remind himself to control his breathing. The doors seemed like they were taking ages to open.

"Wait for the all-clear," Harvey reminded them.

As soon as the doors finished opening, Harvey stomped on the gas. He sped up the ramp and emerged onto the lunar surface. Turning the corner around the garage, he immediately saw a pack member crawling toward him. Sanjay had hypothesized that the werewolves still possessed some form of senses even in the vacuum of space. The hope was that setting off the airlock alarms would be like ringing the dinner bell. Harvey jerked out of the way, almost losing control in the process. He considered running the beast over but didn't want to risk crashing so soon. *I have to get them as far from base as possible,* he thought. Harvey turned his head to see that he was now being chased by the two smaller werewolves.

"Rover One, this is Rover Two. I got the two pups on my tail, but I'm still not seeing the big guy."

That quickly changed as Harvey turned the corner on Armstrong Base and saw Popov leaping through the air. The good doctor landed right on the front of the rover and immediately tried to swipe at Harvey. Luckily, he was able to duck in time and the swipe just barely missed. A giant claw came down on Harvey's shoulder. Harvey looked up and saw that he was now face-to-face with Popov. The rover was still in motion, but Popov didn't seem to care. He smiled at Harvey and was about to take a bite of his skull before Harvey swerved once more. This caused the big creature to almost fall off, although he regained his grip and came back up to meet his prey. That was when he saw that Harvey was now aiming a gun at his face.

"Got ya, fucker!"

Harvey pulled the trigger of the flare gun. The flare didn't ignite, but it lodged itself right in the werewolf's eye socket. Popov recoiled in pain and lost his grip, falling hard on the lunar surface.

I can't believe that actually worked!

They didn't have anything close to a gun on the Moon, which meant the crew had to get creative with their weapons. When it was decided that Harvey would be the one to lead the charge, he knew that he wanted something that would at least hurt the creatures if they got too close. He just never expected the flare gun to work so well. Harvey increased his speed and turned back to see that all three pack members were now chasing him. The shot to the eye had clearly enraged Popov, who was now baring his teeth with every stride. Harvey had no doubt that if he could hear anything, it would be bloodcurdling growls. It was the one time that he was thankful for being in a vacuum.

"I got them all! Move, guys! Go! Go! Go!"

That was all the motivation Jessica needed as she started their climb up the garage ramp. Like Harvey, she sped up as soon as the rover's tires got onto the surface. As they raced away from Armstrong Base, Jessica looked over and saw Rover Two and the massive dust cloud in its wake. By her guess, Harvey was almost doing 50 MPH right now. The fact that he hadn't wrecked had been an absolute miracle. *Maybe he does actually know what he's doing,* she thought.

I have no idea what the fuck I'm doing, Harvey thought. Harvey's plan was simple:

Step one: piss off the werewolves and get them to chase him.

Step two: lead them far away so that the crew could get to the shuttle.

Step three: kill all the werewolves, save the crew, and write a best-selling novel about it later.

Step one was successful so far.

Harvey shot another flare at a pack chasing him. He had no idea if he hit any of them or not, he was just trying to keep their attention. Truthfully, he'd never expected to even get this far. Harvey was doing his best to avoid any rocks or craters, but it was getting harder and harder with the pack gaining on him. Despite that Harvey was now pushing 60 MPH, the wolves showed no sign of slowing down. They were running on all-fours, snarling and drooling. Harvey didn't want to think about what they were going to do once they caught him.

He saw the dust kick up from the other rover off in the distance. It looked like the crew were making their way to the shuttle. *Perfect, I just need to get a little farther.* Harvey was trying to reload when one of the wolves hit the rear of the rover. The sudden jolt caused Harvey to drop the flare gun and try to regain control of the steering wheel. He turned to see one of the smaller wolves coming up on his side.

"Come on, puppies. Come and get me," he taunted, feeling like a badass for only a few seconds. Suddenly, Popov was running alongside the passenger side, and Harvey no longer felt like a badass.

The wolf stared at Harvey with rage and hunger. He ran into the rover, driving his shoulder into it. Harvey was barely able to keep it from swerving into a nearby crater. He pulled up the flare gun that had fallen to the floor, firing it at him once more. The doctor let out a yelp as the flare hit his shoulder. This sent him tumbling back to the hard ground.

Harvey turned to see the horizon just in time to see the large rock formation in front of the rover. He swerved at the last minute, but the tire still hit it too hard, launching Harvey and the rover. Harvey was able to jump free at the last minute. Although it didn't help much, he was able to hit the ground a little lighter than the rover. Harvey immediately tried getting to his feet, but one of his legs wouldn't work. Try as he might, it looked like the best he could do was stand on one foot. One of the wolves was already on him, lunging at his throat. Harvey ducked just in time and grabbed a nearby rock. He needed a weapon, and this was the best he had at the moment. As he stood up, a large paw hit him from the side, knocking him down. Popov stood over him, the flare still sticking out of his eye. It looked like it was stuck in there with coagulated blood.

This looks like it's going to hurt, Harvey though as Popov brought his paw up, uppercutting Harvey across the face. There was a crack in his helmet now. Air was coming out.

It won't be much longer...

"Harvey, give us an update. How are you doing out there?" He heard the commander's voice.

"I've been better, Commander. Doesn't look like I'm going to be lasting much longer out here. You guys need to hurry."

The wolves were snarling as they clawed and kicked his defenseless body. One of them gave Harvey a kick right to the stomach that sent him careening into a boulder a few feet away.

As he started to look up again, Popov was ripping the flare from his eye, grinding his teeth as he did so. He looked to the other two werewolves now circling their prey, waiting for their leader to make the first move. Popov raised his massive claw and swiped at Harvey to deliver the finishing blow—only for it to be stopped. Much to the shock of Popov and the other wolves, Harvey held the massive claw in his hand. The moment of confusion was just the opening he needed. He pulled the doctor in close and punched him in the gut, clearly hurting him. Another punch to the face sent him sprawling to the ground. The other two wolves now pounced on Harvey, not willing to give him a moment of reprieve. They were significantly smaller than Popov but still powerful. The first one lunged at his leg while the second jumped on his back. They pushed him back to the ground, slicing at his air pack as they went.

"Commander, it looks like this is it."

Harvey saw Popov lumbering toward him. He tore the wolf off Harvey's back and grabbed him by the shoulder, lifting Harvey with one hand. Popov brought Harvey close so that he could look directly into his eyes. It was clear that he was done playing with his food when he impaled his other claw right through Harvey's gut. Harvey looked down only to see that Popov's arm had gone clear through his abdomen.

Popov grinned. This was just the first meal of many more to come, he knew. But as he pulled his claw from the astronaut's stomach, there was no blood. Instead, it was covered in...oil? Popov looked up at Harvey's face and pulled his helmet off. Where he hoped would be meat and bone, there was metal. In Popov's grasp was none other than HOGAN. The android's emoticon showed a surprised face.

(˚ O ˚)

"Commander, they're on to me!" Harvey yelled.

Popov dug his claws in deeper to the android and roared. He knew that he had been duped, but in his rage, he failed to notice the danger he was now in. HOGAN's face switched one last time.

凸(¬‿¬)

"This is for Mike, you son of a bitch!" Harvey said as he pressed the trigger from the safety of Rover One. A white light flashed, and the explosion ignited, engulfing HOGAN and the werewolves with it.

14

"I got them!" Harvey shouted from the back of Rover One. The excited astronaut slid his system-linked visor off his helmet so he could look at his teammates. Harvey was expecting some sort of praise for his efforts, but the crew was too fixated on the actual explosion off the horizon.

Unlike in the movies, a real explosion in space wasn't this big, impressive thing. In fact, there wasn't even sound or fire for that matter. The explosion Harvey created still had some kick to it, though. Rover Two had been loaded with enough combustibles to demolish a small space station.

Harvey had gotten the idea to use HOGAN after Jessica's story. HOGAN wasn't reliable when it came to walking so the decision was made to have him drive, something no one was sure he would be able to do. NASA was vehemently opposed to his idea at

first. Sanders and Vince were able to convince them after speaking to HOGAN's programming team. Vince was able to have them develop a patch that helped improve HOGAN's basic motor responsiveness. He would still be pretty useless if he had to walk, but the patch would help with Harvey's plan. He knew that he needed to get the pack far enough from Armstrong Base so that HOGAN could detonate with minimal risk to everyone else.

Harvey had also filled Rover Two with whatever tools he could find. If it looked sharp, pointy, or like a good blunt object, it went into the rover.

The other unique thing about an explosion in space was the flow of kinetic energy. Because there was hardly any gravity, there was almost nothing weighing down any of the projectiles. This meant that whenever something was sent flying through space, it maintained its momentum until it hit something. So, all of the dangerous tools Harvey loaded into Rover Two acted as deadly projectiles should the force of the blast not do the trick.

"Good work, Harv. Mike would be proud," Sanders said. Before Harvey could tell her thank you, she continued. "Alright, team, hopefully, that takes care of our unwelcome guests, but I don't want us taking any chances. As soon as we get to the shuttle, I want us to treat this like a NASCAR pit stop. Get everything loaded and checked. I want us ready for launch in no less than thirty minutes. Everyone understand?"

In near unison, the crew answered, "Yes, ma'am!"

"And, Harvey, I don't want these things getting the jump on us. Get some of the other rovers in the vicinity to head over to the blast site. I'm not taking any chances with them regenerating or whatever other bullshit happens in the movies."

"Already on it, Commander," Harvey replied as he began entering commands into the computer on his wrist.

One of the handy features of the crew's suit was the ability to take control of any nearby rover. Each rover had its own specialized channel that could be accessed using the communications systems throughout the Moon. This allowed anyone to access any nearby rovers and have them accomplish certain tasks, usually only simple things like giving the team a live feed or collecting rock samples. Although anyone could access this feature, Harvey implemented a rule early into their mission that only allowed him access. This came after Mike had somehow managed to break three rovers in two days. He swore he was only trying to use them for collecting rock samples, but Harvey had his doubts. The doubts were confirmed when he saw Mike and Jessica using the rovers as battle-bots.

The five rovers that Harvey had sent towards the blast site pinged him right as the crew was coming up to the shuttle. Harvey opened the live feed, and it began to play in the corner of his visor. The feed shown from the rover looked like a scene from John Carpenter's *The Thing*. Scattered around what remained of Rover Two were the charred and dismembered remains of the pack. Harvey came upon the pieces of the two smaller wolves first. They each wore a look of terror and disbelief on what remained of their faces. Simmons—or the thing wearing Simmons's uniform, at least—even had a saw blade stuck in the side of his face. After switching between feeds, Harvey could see that the smaller pack members were peppered with rocks and tools. Although that made him happy, it wasn't what he was looking for.

"Where the hell are you?" he mumbled to himself before finally seeing his prize on the feed. Off in the distance, Harvey saw the large, dismembered head of Dr. Popov. Where Simmons and Banks looked terrified, Popov's face had a look of anger. The blast perfectly captured the doctor's final moments when he realized he'd been beat. All that remained of the large werewolf was the upper right side of his torso. It appeared that he had been split in two right below his navel. As the rover scanned down the big wolf, it showed what remained of HOGAN. HOGAN's head and a few wires were clenched in Popov's claws. The android displayed his failure emoticon across his face in red lettering, indicating that his systems were about to go offline.

"Good night, sweet prince," Harvey said quietly.

He had a strange mix of emotions about this whole situation. On the one hand, he'd hated HOGAN with an intense passion. On the other, messing with the android was one of the crew's favorite pastimes. He was a large part of what brought the crew together in the first place. For a moment, Harvey even thought of paying homage to the android by naming his firstborn son Hogan. This was a thought he quickly abandoned when he remembered just how hard the android had made his job these last few months.

Rover One had just arrived at the shuttle when Harvey showed the rest of the crew the carnage from the blast.

"Guys, check it out!" Harvey swiped at his wrist and brought up the live feed to everyone else's screens.

"Good riddance!" said Jessica.

"Good stuff. Now, let's get moving, people! Remember, thirty minutes and we are off the ground," Sanders ordered.

The next few minutes could only be described as organized chaos. The team had spent the last couple of days preparing for this mission. They had rehearsed every aspect of their launch down to the last detail, and each member of the team had a role to play. Luckily for Harvey, his role was mostly complete. He spent his time helping wherever he could while periodically checking in on the feed. He had been checking it every four minutes like clockwork. Everything remained the same each time. The werewolves were dead and what remained of them had been spread across the lunar surface.

The white shuttle stood upright at just over twenty-five feet tall. Harvey and Sanjay were loading what few supplies they had into the bottom. Greg and Commander Sanders were inside the shuttle troubleshooting the systems and making sure everything was working at an optimal level. Jessica was doing her exterior checks, making sure that there was no potential damage. The team was worried that detonating so close to the shuttle might have it hit with some debris but thankfully, everything looked to be intact.

"All right, team, how are we looking out there?" Sanders called over their channel.

Sanjay, Harvey, and Jessica each gave their section a quick once-over before giving each other a thumbs-up.

"Looks like we are good out here, Commander. No visible damage from the blast or asteroid strikes," Jessica reported.

"Good enough for government work. You three get in here. We launch to Gateway in fifteen minutes."

Harvey continued to check the feed like a man possessed. Each time he checked, he expected to see something: a random movement, one of their heads winking or even just one of the bodies missing altogether. But every time he checked, he saw none of those things. The wolves looked dead, their last moments of horror and rage frozen on their faces. After a few checks, Harvey was finally starting to let himself believe that they had done it. The werewolves were dead, and they had won.

The team was getting situated in their seats. Unlike the shuttle they'd taken from Earth, this shuttle was fairly bare bones. It was durable enough, sure, but it wasn't nearly as cumbersome as the one needed to break Earth's atmosphere. These lunar shuttles had been used and reused by NASA for the last few missions. The one they were using was about to depart the Moon for the sixth time.

Commander Sanders began to flip switches on the command console, and the team was relieved to hear the shuttle systems begin to hum.

"Gateway, this is Armstrong Shuttle, how do you read?" the commander called. A few tense seconds of silence followed before the Gateway crew finally responded.

"Armstrong Shuttle, this is Gateway. We have you so loud and so clear, and we cannot wait for you to join us in the next few minutes," Captain Amelia Ortiz, Gateway's second-in-command, replied. The rest of the Gateway crew could be heard in the background cheering in anticipation.

"Please make sure that your crew is securely fastened, that your systems are in the green, and lastly, that you do not have any unwanted pets traveling with you." The joke caused a light chuckle for everyone on board the shuttle. The last few days had been so surreal for everyone. Harvey just couldn't believe that in the next fifteen minutes, they would be home free. This nightmare that had taken his best friend's life and forever altered missions to the Moon was about to be over.

For the first time, Harvey allowed himself to feel a sense of relief. In just a few short moments, it would all be over. He could go back to Earth and deal with the small army of scientists and politicians that were no doubt waiting to question the mission and how his actions aided or hindered the team. He would get to pay his respects to

Mike's family and let them know that he died a hero, saving all of them in the process. He felt a sense of pride knowing that he was the one that came up with a plan to blow up the werewolves, avenging Mike's death in the process. Hell, maybe he would actually write a book or get a movie deal about this whole ordeal. Harvey Howlett, the werewolf slayer. He could get a nice mansion and marry some pretty, young, dumb thing, living out the rest of his days recounting this crazy mission.

As he thought about his make-believe future, he knew that he didn't want to really do any of those things. Right now, he wanted nothing more than to get back to Earth and hug his parents. Jessica reached over from her seat and gripped Harvey's hand. He looked back at her and wondered what else the future held. He was definitely attracted to Jessica, but these last few years have been confusing. They spent the first two years together in training with NASA constantly reminding them that no romance was allowed, because doing so would affect the team dynamics and the integrity of the mission. Still, during these last few years, they had grown close. For a time, Harvey considered her no different than a sister, but that wasn't the case anymore. The way she had been there for him during Mike's death and everything afterwards had meant the world to him. Harvey deeply cared for Jessica. The question was, did she feel the same? That was something he hoped to find out once they were home.

The commander's voice snapped him back to reality.

"Fuck, what is that?"

Harvey instinctively went to bring up the rover feed before he realized that the commander wasn't talking about the wolves. Harvey looked at the center console and saw the words "System Error" flashing in big red lettering over the main screen.

"If it's not one thing then it's another," said an exasperated Jessica.

Dr. Holstrom touched the flashing screen, which brought up a map of the shuttle. Most of it was illuminated in neon green, with the exception of a large red X near the middle of the interior.

"It looks like it's an electrical short of some sort," Holstrom said.

"Fuck! Harvey?" Sanders began, but Harvey was already standing up.

"I'm on it. Don't worry, guys, just know that I expect full credit for getting our asses off the Moon in one piece."

Harvey pushed himself out of his chair and glided down to the area indicated on the screen. He lifted the side paneling and pulled out the wires that needed repair. After a quick examination, Harvey was able to diagnose the problem. He was a few minutes into his repairs when a panicked Dr. Holstrom called him.

"How long does it take to fix a simple wiring issue?"

Before Harvey could snap at him, Commander Sanders spoke.

"Harvey, I'm not trying to rush you, but can you give us a timetable? If we don't launch in the next few minutes, we will miss our rendezvous with Gateway. We will have to wait another two hours before they orbit over us again."

"Well, Greg's shitty attitude added a few seconds, but I'm almost done," Harvey replied as he finished his task. A couple minutes later, he placed the mess of wires back into the panel and closed it.

Harvey pushed himself up and used the lack of gravity to easily glide back to his seat.

"Alright, Commander, try it now."

Harvey swung himself around into his chair. Commander Sanders entered her commands on the keyboard for a system's check. To everyone's relief, the screen came back with no error codes. The crew cheered in celebration, with Sanjay surprisingly being the loudest. Sanders keyed up on the frequency to the station once more.

"Gateway, we're coming to you. Start the countdo—"

The commander stopped short when something hit the outside of the shuttle. It was enough force to make the crew jerk forward in their seats. Before anyone could ask what was going on, another impact hit the opposite side. Alarms blared, and a red screen flashed on the center console with the words "Engine Damaged, Check Engine" repeatedly.

"Is it asteroids?" Sanjay asked, hoping that his worst fears hadn't been realized. Harvey was frantically trying to pull the rover feed up when he heard Jessica answer Sanjay.

"No..." she whispered.

Harvey raised his head to see his greatest fear standing outside the shuttle. Popov was standing tall just a few feet away from them. What remained of his EVA suit had been torn away thanks to HOGAN's bomb. The massive wolf stood before the crew, his face a contorted mess of rage and pain. His body was covered in gray fur and fresh crimson scars. He was still putting himself back together, which was obvious when his small intestines slowly started to crawl back into his stomach. His body was expelling the shrapnel as he stood deep in his focus.

"What is he doing?" Holstrom asked.

"He looks like he's healing," Harvey answered as the large creature pulled a chunk of metal from his snout and the wound began to close.

Everyone seemed fixated on Popov, except for Sanders, who was frantically flipping switches and pressing buttons on the console.

"No, no, no," she muttered, slamming her fists onto the console.

Popov stared at the crew. It wasn't like last time, when he looked at them like playthings or food. This time was different. This time, he was pissed. He howled, and the shuttle took another hit. Harvey could hear something crawling on the outside of the metallic shell.

"Armstrong Shuttle, this is Gateway, come in. Armstrong Shuttle, does anybody copy?"

Harvey heard the bottom of the shuttle tearing open.

"Fuck, something just got in!" Jessica shouted. The crew looked to the bottom of the shuttle. One of the exterior hatches must have been torn open. The interior hatch to the main fuselage was still closed.

"Alright, look, it's risky, but we can still do this. I'm launching," Sanders announced.

The crew felt a hard impact from the front. The commander turned, coming face-to-face with Popov, who was now latched to the front of the shuttle. The doctor punched the reinforced glass with all his might and before Commander Sanders knew what was going on, it was already too late. The massive claw grabbed her, digging his nails into her slow enough that she knew she was trapped. The pain was excruciating as she felt her skin stretch and rip. Her screams were deafening. Everything was happening so fast. Lieutenant Colonel Samantha Sanders—decorated soldier, veteran of hundreds of flying missions, devoted wife and amazing mother to three boys, a woman who had faced her demons and didn't so much as wince—was now reduced to a screaming maniac just trying to grab onto something or someone for dear life. That was the crew's first realization. The second one came when they realized that in her painful writhing, she had initiated the launch sequence override. This meant that the crew only had a few seconds before the shuttle launched sky-high toward Gateway.

Harvey started to run to Commander Sanders, to try and help her however he could, but he was stopped by a pull on his arm. Jessica had grabbed him and was pulling him away. Harvey tried to resist before he saw it was too late. The commander's suit was breached at multiple points. Even if they could get her free, she would die in a matter of seconds. The fact that she wasn't already dead was a testament to the woman's toughness. Harvey saw Popov punch another claw through the front of the shuttle, shattering the remaining windshield. He didn't seem to care about the rest of the crew, though. His attention was squarely on Sanders. To her credit, she looked like she was trying to fight off the pack leader. True to her nature, she would fight until the end.

Harvey was yanked through the side of the shuttle door. After falling for what seemed like too long, he hit the jagged lunar surface. During the chaos, Holstrom had stood up and opened the shuttle's emergency hatch. The hatch was located close enough to the cockpit that the crew could make a last-ditch effort in case of something like a fire, or in this case, werewolves.

As soon as Harvey hit the ground, he knew he only had a few seconds to get away from the shuttle before it blasted into orbit. He didn't dare look back, even though he wanted to. He was bringing up the rear with Jessica ahead of him. Sanjay and Holstrom were somehow leading the group. The crew was running as fast as they could when a powerful force hit them from behind. Harvey instinctually got into the fetal position at first but eventually turned to look up. The shuttle, along with Popov and Commander Sanders, had launched. It was immediately obvious that it wasn't flying how it should.

Probably because of the giant fucking hole in the front of it, Harvey thought. After only a few seconds of being airborne, the shuttle started to curve. It wasn't until it was too late that Harvey realized what was happening.

"It's coming right at us!" he yelled.

15

The shuttle careened straight toward the fleeing astronauts. As the vessel cut in, Harvey could still see parts of Popov and Sanders wrestling each other toward the front. The approaching ship was somehow the slowest and fastest thing Harvey had ever seen. He started to run to his right only to look back and see that the shuttle had seemingly changed course. It was flying straight at him again. He corrected and ran to his left only for it to change course once more. It was like a heat-seeking missile, and Harvey was the target. In a moment of clarity, he realized that the shuttle wasn't following him. It was just getting bigger as it got closer. Harvey eventually stopped looking back at the shuttle and just decided to commit to one direction for an all-out sprint. He felt the ground begin to shake before being knocked off his feet. As Harvey rattled through the air, his only thought was to protect himself. He needed to try to steady himself so that his suit wouldn't get damaged. His arm hit the lunar surface hard enough that it instantly went numb. He tried to grab onto anything with his good arm but was unable to do so. The force of the shuttle crash had sent the astronaut into an uncontrollable spiral.

Harvey finally came to a stop after almost fifty feet. He was able to use both arms to get to his feet, despite his left still being numb.

Not a horrible sign, he thought. He started to check his suit for any cuts or breaks but stopped as soon as he saw the wreckage. Had he been standing just a few feet to the left, the shuttle would have splattered him on impact. Harvey followed the skid marks left in the lunar surface and saw that things had somehow just gotten worse. The back portion of the shuttle had hit the ground hard enough to scatter the remaining crew members. The front of the shuttle had skipped like a rock on water, straight into Armstrong Base. Whatever possible hope Harvey and the rest of the crew had for finding shelter was now gone. Harvey stared at the remains of the place that he had called home for these last few months. Whatever life supplies had remained there were now destroyed. The front of the shuttle had torn right through the structure, creating an impressive crater in the process. Harvey started to wonder about the commander and Popov when a grunt over the team's frequency caught his attention. The grunt had come from Sanjay, who was kneeling just a few feet away. Harvey rushed to help him up. Sanjay didn't thank Harvey. Instead, he asked a simple question.

"Where are they?"

"I'm not sure, man. I lost sight of Jessica and—"

"The wolves, Harvey! Where are the wolves?" Sanjay interrupted.

Harvey had been so shaken up by the crash that he'd almost forgotten about the werewolves. Both men's ears perked up when they heard heavy panting. They looked across the shuttle wreckage and saw someone running toward Rover One. Neither needed to guess to know who it was. The labored breathing gave it away.

"Greg! Greg, over here!" Harvey yelled. Holstrom didn't so much as look at Harvey or Sanjay.

"Greg, wait!" came a shriek. Harvey looked over to see Jessica limping behind Holstrom.

"I'm sorry, oh, God, I'm so sorry, Jessica!" Greg replied.

That was when Harvey saw them. Running behind Jessica was one of the werewolves. He was running on all-fours, wearing tatters of his orange jumpsuit.

"Jessica! Behind you!" Harvey yelled. She must have already known that he was after her. Harvey's only thought was that he had to get to her. It was clear even over the distance between them that

Jessica was in incredible pain. Harvey instinctually started to move toward her, but Sanjay stopped him.

"What the fuck, man! She needs us!" Harvey yelled, but Sanjay's grip only tightened.

Jessica was gaining on Dr. Holstrom. Had her leg not been hurt, she would've easily made it to the rover before him. The pain in her leg was excruciating. The shuttle crash had sent her flying into a rock formation. It was amazing enough that her suit hadn't been breached. Greg had started to help her up when they saw the were-wolf appear out of the wreckage. The sight of the creature had sent them both running. Jessica had fallen as soon as she tried to push off her leg. Greg turned to her, looking like he would help her. Instead, he looked at her, then at the creature chasing them, and his mind was made up. Jessica knew that if she was going to make it to the rover, she would have to push it. Right now, she was at the man's mercy. If he would just wait a second for her to jump in the rover, they could drive off and circle back for Harvey and Sanjay.

"Greg... Don't leave me! Greg!" Jessica pleaded but to no avail. Dr. Holstrom was already getting into Rover One.

"I'm so sorry. Fuck, I'm so sorry, Jessica. Just hide, please! Go to Aldrin Base. I'll get us help and come back for all of you, just get to Aldrin Base!" Greg said between his heavy breathing. Jessica was just a few feet away when Dr. Holstrom started Rover One.

Just a few more steps, she thought. She could practically touch it. *I'm going to do it! I'm going to make it!* She reached out to grab onto the rover and felt its metal frame against her glove. As she started to tighten her grip, she noticed that her hand was empty and Rover One was driving away. Jessica fell to her knees, her momentum knocking her off balance.

"I'm so sorry, please, I'm sorry, Jessica," a sobbing Greg said. His pleas cut off by his high-pitched scream when a second werewolf appeared in front of Rover One. Greg narrowly avoided the creature, swerving out of its way at the last minute. The werewolf swiped at Greg but missed his target. Clearly frustrated, the werewolf started to chase the rover.

"Greg, you coward, you just killed us all," she whispered. Jessica's world began to darken as a predator's shadow appeared over top of her. She looked up to see the sinister yellow eyes of Captain Micah Simmons. The captain had a monstrous grin, which showed his jagged teeth with the dried blood of Dr. Chang. Jessica promised herself that she wouldn't scream, that she wouldn't give him the satisfaction. As the former captain lunged at Astronaut Jessica Peoples, she tried to imagine she was someplace else. She thought about her parents and their farm. She imagined seeing them once again. She thought about her dog Bogey. She had left him with her parents during her training. The last time she'd seen him, it was evident that her mother had been feeding Bogey one too many helpings of dinner. She thought about her team and how she had grown to love this group of strangers over the last few years. She thought about the many late-night talks, the laughs, the tears, the ups, and the downs. She thought about Harvey and then she thought about the what-could've-beens. She thought about whatever she could so that she could drown out the sound of her screams as Captain Simmons tore into her flesh. Nothing she thought would change the fact that his face—his sick, grinning face—would be the last thing she ever saw.

"No!" Harvey screamed.

Sanjay kept his grip as best he could, but Harvey's anger was too much. He finally broke free and started to run toward Jessica. He had no plan. He only knew that he was going to kill the wolf or die trying. Sanjay grabbed Harvey once more and pulled him back.

"We need to get to Aldrin Base, Harvey, it's our only chance." Harvey didn't seem to hear his friend's pleas. He was too caught up in his anger. Sanjay tried once more. "Dammit, Harvey, she's dead! Jessica is dead!"

That was enough to stop Harvey in his tracks. He wanted nothing more than to charge over to the feeding werewolf and fight it to the bitter end, but he knew Sanjay was right. Jessica's screams had finally stopped. He knew that he couldn't save her. Tears started to well in Harvey's eyes.

"Come on, we need to go. If not for me then do it for her. She would want you to live, so live Harvey!"

"Shit," he muttered before turning back to Sanjay.

They started running toward Aldrin Base. Pain shot up Harvey's leg with each stride. Luckily for him, the base was less than a mile from their present location.

Unfortunately, the werewolf that had been feeding on Jessica had just finished his meal. He picked her clean, leaving nothing to waste, and yet he was still starving. He needed to feast and soon, the hunger demanded it, Lycaon demanded it. He looked in the direction that his brother had run off in. He could catch up, of course, but what if his brother had already caught his prey? What if there was nothing left for him? He looked around for other prey. *The shuttle couldn't have killed them all,* he thought. That was when he saw them: the two little things running toward his base. He smiled and gave chase. He would feast upon this new prey and inherit their gifts, then he would be the alpha.

———

Harvey and Sanjay were coming up to the bent doors of Aldrin Base. Their lungs burned, and their legs were numb. The two said nothing as they opened the airlock doors. They knew they only had a little time to get a new air supply. They had used up so much of their current air cannisters in the last hour. If they didn't find a new supply soon, it wouldn't matter if the wolves got to them or not.

The airlock doors started to shut behind them. Harvey looked at Sanjay and let out a sigh of relief before the doors came to a grinding halt. Harvey looked down and saw a pair of bloodied claws pulling them open.

"Fuck!" Sanjay yelled.

"Get to the infirmary," Harvey said as the two men started running through the corridor. Harvey heard the airlock slam open behind him followed by the sound of nails running on metal. As Sanjay turned the corner, Harvey felt a sharp pain in his foot just before he was yanked off his feet.

Fuck! Not again!

He rolled onto his back to see the large werewolf standing over him. Harvey was terrified at first. When he realized that it was the same wolf that had killed Jessica, his fear quickly turned to anger. He punched at the werewolf with all his might, hitting him in the jaw, causing the beast to recoil. Harvey clenched his fist once more and punched at the monster again, only this time, his fist landed right into the creature's mouth. Harvey's anger quickly turned to pain as he felt the werewolf's teeth clench around his hand, breaking his bones as the jaws tightened. The creature started to shake Harvey's arm like he was trying to rip it off. Harvey started to scream when he heard his tendons rip and his bones crack. The monster seemed to relish every second of his agony.

Harvey began hitting the wolf with his other arm but could tell that his strength was fading fast. He tried to think of something, anything he could do to at least cause more pain to this thing, but it was no use. Harvey was struggling just to keep his eyes open as the werewolf thrashed on top of him. His vision was starting to fade when he was jolted awake by what sounded like a chainsaw. He opened his eyes only to see Sanjay running at him with a giant electric saw. The werewolf started to lunge at Sanjay but was met with the saw's blade. Sanjay let out a primal yell as he brought the saw down further into the yelping monster's body. Blood erupted from the creature's neck and fell onto Harvey, who was trying his best to crawl away from the monster. As he reached for something to steady himself, Harvey felt something familiar on the floor, causing him to grin.

Sanjay continued battling the beast with the surgical saw. Despite the monster's throat having been cut, it was still doing its best to fight, swiping its remaining claw at Sanjay, knocking him over in the process. It seemed like the wolf was about to pounce on his adversary. That was until Harvey stabbed a screwdriver into the monster's leg, bringing it to one knee. The wolf grabbed at the fading Harvey only for Sanjay to take advantage of the opening. The saw blade rang as it cut clean through what remained of the monster's neck. Its pitiful yelps were drowned out by Harvey and Sanjay's incoherent shouting. Harvey kept stabbing wildly into the creature until he felt its body go limp. The werewolf's head fell into Harvey's lap, looking up at him in horror. Harvey looked up at Sanjay, the two men exhausted from their ordeal. Panting heavily, Sanjay gave him a nod and Harvey raised his hand.

"High-five, man."

Only for him to see his mangled arm covered in blood. His hand, or at least what remained of it, was hanging on by just a few pieces of skin.

"Oh... Well, that sucks," Harvey said before he passed out from his blood loss.

16

Harvey could feel the earth beneath his feet as he chased after his prey. He ran through the forest, dodging every branch as he tried to keep up with the rabbit in front of him. The creature had been eluding him for too long. As he came around the path, he saw that the rabbit was now running toward the cave. Harvey's two legs weren't cutting it, so he dropped to all-fours and began running faster. He was gaining on his prey now, but he worried it was too late. If the rabbit got to the cave, it would all be over. Instinct took over as Harvey leapt through the air and came crashing down on the vermin. He bit into the rabbit's neck, making the creature let out a sickly scream. He tore away from its neck, taking blood and tendons with him. When he looked down, the rabbit had disappeared and now a bloodied Jessica lay in its place.

Harvey stood up in shock, mortified at what he had just done. He wanted to scream but couldn't. Now that he thought about it, he couldn't even breathe. The forest disappeared around him, and the dirt beneath his feet turned to lunar dust. Harvey walked naked on the Moon looking for someone, anyone, that could help him. *It wasn't my fault,* he thought. *I didn't mean to hurt her, to hurt them. I am just so scared, so scared and so hungry.* Harvey struggled to walk, each step a reminder that he couldn't breathe. The coldness of space was affecting him. He needed air, air and warmth, but first he needed food. As he continued his laborious walk, he saw a large Greek temple in front of him. Even from this distance, he could see that there were people there. People and a fire. Every step he took toward the marble structure became easier and easier. Harvey could see a long, empty wooden table within the temple. With every step, Harvey could feel the warmth returning to his body. He could feel the air returning to his lungs little by little. The only thing that had not changed was the pit in his stomach. Finally, as Harvey took his first step onto the marble floors of the temple, he felt his strength return to him like a tidal wave. No longer was he cold or struggling to breathe.

"Ah, good! Good! We are so pleased that you are here!"

Harvey looked up at a regal man standing in front of him. The man was dressed in golden robes with a golden leaf crown atop his head.

"Who are you?" Harvey asked, except no words came out of his mouth.

"Why, I am King Lycaon, of course. This is my temple, and you are my most honored guest. Please, won't you come sit and eat with us?" King Lycaon gestured to the large table.

"Us?" Harvey looked over to see that the once barren table was now covered in an elaborate feast. A seemingly endless amount of dinner guests now sat around the table, laughing and drinking. Each guest wore pristine decorative robes, though none were as extravagant as King Lycaon's.

Harvey was sitting at one end of the table now. The laughing and talking had all come to a halt. Everyone was staring at him in anticipation. They all wore the same wide grin. King Lycaon sat at the other end of the table holding a fork and knife.

"What are we waiting for?" Harvey asked.

"We are waiting for you, of course. You are our honored guest; it is you that must take the first bite." King Lycaon extended his hand, gesturing toward a dinner plate in front of Harvey. Harvey hadn't realized that it had been there this entire time. Lying on his plate was a partially cooked, bloodied rabbit. Harvey looked around at the other guests, each nodding in approval. He looked back to King Lycaon, who seemed slightly gaunter than before. *This isn't right,* Harvey thought before looking back down at his plate. His stomach ached with insatiable hunger, and the rabbit was impossible to resist. Harvey grabbed the vermin and bit into it, feeling its blood roll down his chin. He'd never tasted anything so sweet, so delicious. He heard rumblings around the table, no doubt the other dinner guests sharing in the feast.

He did not look up until he had picked the rabbit clean to the bone but when he did, he saw that the dinner guests had changed. Where the guests once sat, there were now wolves eating at the table. Each one was ravenous as it devoured the food in front of it. Harvey looked over to King Lycaon, who still appeared human, but something was off about him. As Harvey looked closer, he saw that the still-smiling king was looking more and more like a decomposing corpse as the seconds went by. His hair began to wither, but he was still smiling. His teeth began to rot, but he was still smiling. His skin began to gray and mold, but he was still smiling. Even as his yellow eyes turned to goo, he still smiled at Harvey.

Harvey suddenly felt a searing pain in his arm. He screamed and this time, he could hear himself. He raised his head to see Sanjay on top of him. The panicked man was looking from Harvey to a beeping monitor.

"You're going to be okay, Harvey! You're going to be okay."

Harvey's vision faded back to black.

He was naked on the moon again, but this time, he wasn't alone. Hundreds of naked people stood around him. They each wore fur pelts wrapped around their heads and shoulders. Everyone was chanting, but Harvey couldn't understand what they were saying. Despite how loud they appeared to be, how forceful they were in their chants, he could not hear them. They were all facing a marble statue on the horizon. Harvey walked cautiously toward the statue that seemed so familiar yet so alien. As he got closer, he could make out its features. The marble statue was that of a beautiful woman wearing a toga. She had a quiver around her back and her hair was a beautiful, wild mess. Her athletic body held a bow in one hand while the other hand reached out welcomingly. Harvey couldn't help but continue to walk toward this beautiful woman who seemed more and more lifelike the closer he got.

"Harvey..." He heard a whisper that sounded like Jessica's voice, but he knew that it wasn't. No, it was somebody else, somebody who was much more important. It was the voice of his goddess, his one and true love. Harvey reached out and grasped the statue's marble hand in his own.

"Artemis..."

Harvey felt like his eardrums were about to rupture. He was suddenly overwhelmed with the sounds of all the chanting and laughing of the naked people around him. He turned to look at them, these people who were more beast than human, chanting in guttural voices: "Lycaon, Lycaon, Lycaon, Lycaon, Lycaon."

Where he once felt comfort, Harvey was now filled with fear. He wanted to run, hide from whatever was coming, but he couldn't. He felt a cold grip tighten around his hand. Harvey turned to see that the once-beautiful statue of Artemis had changed.

The statue now towered over Harvey, its beautiful features now a deformed monstrosity. She stared at him with menacing yellow eyes as she pulled him off the ground. Harvey dangled in the void, his goddess's grip his only safety. The naked people were forming below him now, each one still chanting and laughing. They laughed as the pelts atop their heads overtook their bodies, changing them into chanting werewolves. Each one was reaching for him, pleading for their goddess to release him so they could tear him apart. Harvey looked back to Artemis and pleaded for her not to release him, not to let him go. The goddess stared at him with indifference.

The marble around her face began to crack as her stone lips curved into a sickly smile. Artemis opened her hand, and Harvey fell into the ocean of fur, teeth, and blood. They ripped and tore his body until there was nothing left. Nothing but the blackness.

Harvey could hear the beeping of the EKG monitor as he drifted in and out of consciousness. He attempted to open his eyes a few times, but everything seemed so blurry. He looked around the room, attempting to focus on something while his vision adjusted. He found a dark shape in the white blur of the infirmary. The shape was lying next to him, and it was unmoving. As his vision started to adjust, he was greeted by the severed head of Captain Micah Simmons. Normally, this would have shocked Harvey, but after the dream he'd just had, it seemed quite tame. He sat up on the small bed and began to peel the EKG stickers off his body. He removed the first one with one hand but there was something strange when he tried to reach with the other. He couldn't feel his grip.

Harvey looked down at his hands and began to shout. His right hand, his good hand, was still intact. The left hand, however, was gone. A bandaged, bloodied stump was left in its place. Harvey heard the doors to the infirmary open. Sanjay raced in, power saw in hand. The room started to blur again. Harvey was having difficulty focusing on Sanjay. The power saw in Sanjay's grasp turned into a syringe. He was saying something, but Harvey couldn't understand what. He was trying to force him back on the bed. Harvey's vision was a complete blur as he reached up and grabbed Sanjay by the collar.

"What did you do?" Harvey asked through gritted teeth as he slipped back into unconsciousness.

A few more hours passed before Harvey awoke once more.

Harvey was greeted with the familiar sound of the EKG monitor's beeps, indicating that he was still clinging to life. His vision was still blurry when he looked around the familiar room. The severed were-wolf head that lied next to him was now gone and in its place was a mysterious figure sitting in a chair in the corner. As his vision adjusted, Harvey saw the previously decapitated monster now sitting in the chair. He sat cross-legged as he stared at Harvey with those yellow eyes. There was dried blood around his neck from where they had cut off his head. Harvey blinked and the werewolf disappeared. In his place sat Sanjay.

"Hey, buddy, how you are feeling?"

"What? What happened?" asked a still-groggy Harvey. He started to sit up, which prompted Sanjay to spring out of the chair and rush over to him.

"Easy does it. You've been out for a while. I don't want you making any sudden moves right away."

"How...how long have I been asleep?"

Sanjay stared at Harvey for a few seconds, clearly trying to think of the right words.

"It's been almost three days, man. Although I wouldn't really call what you've been doing sleeping. The first day was rough, to say the least. You had a fever for the last couple days along with what sounded like some pretty intense nightmares."

"Yeah, I think it's safe to say that I developed a whole new set of phobias from this trip."

Harvey turned to stand but was met with resistance. He looked down to see that both of his legs were tied to the bed. He didn't say anything, just nodded at his restraints.

"Yeah, about those. Nothing personal, I just wasn't about to take any chances after everything that happened with Dr. Chang. And look, man, about the hand..." Tears began to well up in Sanjay's eyes. "Harvey, I... I tried, man. Honest to God, I did the best that I could with it, but it was so mangled. A lot of the equipment needed for proper surgery looked like it was damaged or missing. I didn't have a lot of options and..."

"Sanjay! It's okay, man, I know that you did the best you could. You and I've seen more than enough creature features to know what a bite from a werewolf does to you. We both saw what happened to Dr. Chang. I'll be upset about not being able to juggle later, but for right now, I'm just grateful that you were here, man. I would've died back there without you, so please trust me when I say that it's fine."

It wasn't fine, but Harvey wasn't about to say that to the already guilt-ridden Sanjay. Harvey had experienced a lot of things these last few days. He had suffered the loss of friends and had faced monsters worse than any nightmare he could have envisioned. Despite all of that, he always maintained the will to live. Now though, for the first time since the initial attack, he felt truly hopeless. His hands were the only thing that made him a contribution to the team. They were the only thing that had helped him survive up until this point. His hands were his God-given gift, and now they were essentially useless. Even if they somehow made it back to Earth, he could never go back to his old life. His passion of tinkering and fixing things was now a thing of the past.

Sanjay began undoing the straps on Harvey's legs.

"I appreciate that, Harvey, and I'm sorry about the restraints. Like I said... After Dr. Chang, I didn't want to take any chances. I hoped to remove the hand in time before any infection could spread, but after some of the noises, you were making...the things you were saying... I thought better safe than sorry."

Harvey tried to remember his dreams, but now it all seemed like a blur. He remembered feeling terror, like he was being chased. Then he remembered feeling powerful, like nothing could stop him. He had the faintest memory of a woman, but he couldn't picture her. The only thing he remembered was the word "Lycaon," but he didn't know why.

"I understand, Sanjay. Honestly, I do. I wish I remembered what I saw, but it's all just a weird fever dream to me now."

Sanjay stared at him for a few more seconds. Whether it was shame from having to amputate his hand or disappointment from not getting any answers about the dreams, Harvey couldn't say.

"Well, you've been out for almost three days. I'm sure that you have a lot of questions, so I might as well give you an update on just how fucked we are. Follow me please."

17

Harvey followed Sanjay into the command center of Aldrin Base. He was surprised to see that not only had Sanjay been able to repair some of the previously broken equipment, but the command center looked immaculate with almost no sign of the carnage that took place just a few days prior.

"Did you... Did you clean?"

"I did the best I could. Honestly, after I cut your hand off, your condition improved. I would check in on you and cleanup in here to kill some time. As odd as it sounds, it was a little bit of a stress relief for me. My parents always kept a clean house."

Sanjay began typing at the main desk of the command center.

"What did you do with the body of the wolf that attacked us?"

"I moved it to another capsule. I tried to clean up as best I could, but we made a hell of a mess. I've been...examining it..."

"And?"

"I'll admit that my knowledge in molecular biology is lacking, but I can say without a shadow of a doubt that these things are unlike anything on Earth."

"Well, no shit, I could've told you that. Were you able to find anything else out about them? Any weaknesses? Fire? Silver? Anything?"

"No... This lab isn't equipped for that type of testing and even if it were, I wouldn't know where to start. This just isn't my field of expertise. I was brought on to study the long-term effects of humans on the lunar surface. I wouldn't know the first place to start for running tests like that. In all honesty, nothing about these things makes any sense. They are covered in fur, but it shouldn't be enough to protect them from the below-freezing temperatures of space. After their mutation is complete, they still possess lungs like any other mammal, but you can't breathe in space. Every one of their traits makes them the perfect predator for a planet like Earth. The only reason that I can think that they are even surviving out there is because they possess some sort of healing factor, which is why I took special care to store the head of the one we killed away from its body."

"Well, does NASA have anything to say about this?"

"Ah, that brings me back to how fucked we are." Sanjay typed a few more commands into the computer before hitting enter. The screens around the command center began to display outside security footage. Standing directly outside of the base were the two remaining members of the pack. The one that had chased after Greg was crouched over on a piece of debris. Standing just a few feet away from him was the unmistakable presence of Dr. Popov. The alpha wolf looked like he had seen better days. What remained of his EVA suit had been completely destroyed along with a majority of the skin on his body, revealing exposed bones and muscles. Despite half his face being skeletal, the doctor still looked like he was wearing that sick grin.

"Communications went out shortly after we got here. I was able to make first contact with Vince and update him on our situation, but I'm guessing one of these guys put a stop to that. I'm not entirely sure when they showed up. I'm not even sure if Greg was able to get away. By the time I was able to get you stabilized, they were already standing outside. They tried to break in the first couple of days, but the security system put a stop to that. It doesn't look like they've moved since yesterday. For right now, it looks like the security system is holding. That's the good news."

"That's the good news?"

"It looks like most this base's supplies were destroyed in the initial explosion. After taking an inventory of what little we have left, we might be able to last for two weeks. And before you ask, that's with rationing."

"Fuck..."

Sanjay was still typing away at the keyboard, seemingly unfazed by their predicament.

"I know, things are pretty bad, but I thought you might find this next bit interesting. Did you guys actually watch any of the footage that you recovered from here?"

"I can't say that we did. We were too busy being creeped out about all of the dead rodents and burnt corpses."

"Oh, that reminds me. Colonel Jackson is missing."

"Missing? Where the fuck did he go?"

"I'm not sure. I just know he hasn't been here since we arrived. Maybe he drifted away or one of the wolves wanted a snack. All I know is that I haven't seen him since I was able to get you stabilized. Anyways, this is what I wanted to show you. It won't answer all of your questions, but it might shed some light on what happened here. I found the thumb drive in your suit. Figured it was either the security footage or a secret stash of movies. Either way, I started looking at these while you were sleep. For the most part, the videos are your typical logs. People are either sending messages to their loved ones or talking about the mission. Then I came across this video and as far as I can tell, this is what started everything."

Sanjay pressed a key and a video began to play on the main screen

[Log11292048/Aldrin/W.Popov]

"Hello, this is Dr. Willhelm Popov of the Artemis Mission Fourteen. The date is Sunday, the twenty-ninth of November. I am here to report that we have made quite an exciting discovery at Aldrin Base. Dr. Chang, if you would please?"

Dr. Popov waved his hand, indicating for Dr. Chang to have the camera zoom out. It was unsettling for Harvey to see Popov as a human again. The man had been so jovial and full of life. He was so kind and would go out of his way to tell people about his research, almost like a schoolteacher instructing children but not in a demeaning way. He always made everyone feel at ease. Now the only trait that he kept from his former self was his large smile, which never seemed to fade. The video began to pan out, showing Dr. Popov standing behind a large lab table with something on top of it. It took a few seconds for Harvey to realize what that something was.

"Are those..."

Harvey's thought was immediately interrupted by the video.

"As you can see, we believe that we have discovered alien bones on the moon. Or more specifically, underneath the Moon. On November twenty-seventh at approximately oh-three-hundred Zulu time, we experienced a small tremor. This tremor opened a previously inaccessible part of the lunar cavern that we had been excavating. At first glance, the cavern appeared to be insignificant, but after careful observation, we were able to find this magnificent specimen. Now, of course we would've liked to have told you about this sooner, but unfortunately, we are in the middle of a very powerful solar storm. Our computer indicates that the storm will pass within the next week. When it does, I'm sure you will see this video log and be overjoyed. On behalf of Aldrin Base, I would just like to say congratulations. Alien life does exist, and it exists on the very moon that we have been looking up at for millions of years. My sincerest thanks to everyone involved."

Dr. Chang and the rest of Aldrin crew began to cheer behind the camera. Dr. Popov had tears welling up in his eyes. He blew a kiss with both of his hands as the video log ended.

"Fucking aliens?" Harvey exclaimed.

"Just wait, there's more. Much more..."

[Log11302048/Aldrin/W.Popov]

.   .   .

125

The video started similarly the last one. Dr. Popov was standing behind the table with the alien bones on it.

"This is Dr. Wilhelm Popov of Aldrin Base. The date is November thirtieth, and the time is oh-four-hundred Zulu. I have taken it upon myself to examine the bones in an attempt to better understand what we are dealing with. While some of my colleagues here may find my methods rash, I assure you I followed all safety protocols and ensured that there are no levels of radiation within these bones. I accept full responsibility for any slight mishap that may result of my tinkering."

"See, this is where it doesn't make any sense. NASA has very specific guidelines on what we are supposed to do if we ever come into contact with anything alien in origin. Those bones shouldn't even be in the facility, let alone out of containment. The fact that he is doing this makes me wonder if he had some sort of hidden agenda," Sanjay said.

"That, or you gotta wonder if Kronos gave him some sort of assurance that nothing would happen to him if he discovered anything like this," Harvey suggested.

Popov held up what looked like a fragment of a jawbone.

"Now, it appears that the aliens had elongated faces similar to that of a dog."

"Or a fucking wolf," Harvey muttered.

Dr. Popov let out a sudden yell and gripped his hand as a familiar crimson began to drip from it.

"My goodness, Doctor, are you okay?" came Chang's voice from behind the camera.

"Yes... Yes, Alana, thank you. I'm okay, just a little cut. Perhaps we should finish our recording for today."

The screen cut to black.

[Log12012048/Aldrin/W. Popov]

Dr. Popov was once again standing behind the lab table with the alien bones. The doctor looked pale and had sweat running down his forehead. The doctor was holding something in his hands. It took Harvey a little bit to realize that it was one of the many lab rats that used to call Aldrin Base home.

"After some further tests, I am excited to say that my suspicions have been confirmed. We have found bone marrow still intact within the specimen. The majority of the marrow has been extracted and properly stored, but I have kept a small portion to run further tests."

"Doctor, if I may? I just... I just don't think that this is the best—"

"You've made your theories well known, Dr. Chang. There's no need to restate them just for the video camera!" Dr. Popov snapped. "History favors the bold, Alana. We have made the most important discovery in the history of mankind. We have the unique—no, the honorable—opportunity to study an alien specimen, and you are cowering away? Do you know how many scientists would kill just to be in your position right now?"

"I just..."

"It's rhetorical, Alana. Now, if you would please shut your mouth and handle the video camera. Apparently, that is all that I can rely on you for."

"Yes, Doctor," Chang said, clearly doing her best to keep her anger in check.

"Now, as I was saying, I have saved some of the bone marrow so that we may run future tests. One of which will be injecting some of that marrow into Eli here." Dr. Popov held up the white rat in his hands. "We have recently discovered traces of cancer in poor Eli's system. While I'm not sure if we can help him, studying the effects of the marrow will help give us a better idea of how these creatures survived in such an inhospitable environment. Thank you, Dr. Chang, you can turn it off now."

"Yes, sir." Dr. Chang pressed a button on the recorder but didn't stop the video from recording.

"Dr. Popov, I was trying to..."

"If you ever contradict me like that again, I will fuck up your world, do you understand me!" Dr. Popov snarled before the screen went to black.

"Holy fuck, that escalated quickly," Harvey said.

"Just wait until you see the next log," Sanjay replied.

[Log12012048/Aldrin/W. Popov]

Harvey heard the loud screeching before he saw anything else on the black screen. The camera started to shake as it was picked up and turned to face Dr. Popov.

"I injected the bone marrow sample into Eli just two hours ago. The cancer cells in his body completely disappeared within the first hour. Unfortunately, he seems to be having some adverse reaction to the injection."

Popov turned the camera to show Eli, who was screaming bloody murder. The poor rat had almost doubled in size and was splayed out on the table.

The creature was pinned onto the table mat with large dissection needles. Poor Eli's organs were on display as he writhed in agony. Despite the immense pain that the rodent must have been in, it seemed more angry than hurt. Every move that Dr. Popov made toward it was met with aggression as Eli tried to bite at the doctor.

"If you look closely, you can see that his lungs have changed so that he—"

Harvey heard the sound of the laboratory door opening. The startled Dr. Popov spun the camera to show Lt. Colonel Jackson, Captain Banks, and Dr. Chang.

"This is a closed laboratory! Do you have any idea what type of risk you pose just by being in here? And you, Dr. Chang, I told you not to—"

"Wilhelm, what the hell are you doing in here? What the fuck are you doing with that animal?" Jackson demanded.

Dr. Popov struggled with the camera for a moment before he unceremoniously put it on the table. The video now showed Popov and Jackson standing next to each other near the table. Harvey could barely see Chang and Banks in the corner of the screen.

"I am trying to do some minor experiments with our findings from the cavern, Colonel. Something that is almost impossible to do with the likes of you contaminating my—"

"Are you shitting me right now? Wilhelm, look at yourself! I don't even know where to begin. When Dr. Chang said that you had been acting funny, I almost didn't believe her, but now... Wilhelm, you're not well, and this proves it. I'm shutting this down, right now."

"Colonel, if you would just let me explain, then I think that—"

"Explain what? For fuck's sake, I can't even hear myself think and you think that I'm going to—"

Without hesitation, Dr. Popov stabbed his scalpel into Eli's skull, killing the rodent and bringing an end to his screams. Before anyone else could do anything, the doctor was standing face-to-face with Jackson and had grabbed his collar.

"No one is shutting me down! Not NASA and sure as hell not you, Scott!"

Lt. Colonel Jackson stared down at Dr. Popov.

"Wilhelm... I'm going to tell you this once. Let go of me."

Jackson's cold response seemed to return Dr. Popov to his senses. He let go of the colonel's collar and brought his gaze to the floor in shame.

"I'm sorry, Scott. I... I don't know what I was thinking. I think... I think I need some rest."

"You can rest after we talk. Right now, I think that we need to discuss a few things."

The camera kept recording as the group walked out the laboratory. Sanjay had the video fast-forward to a couple of hours later. Dr. Popov walked into laboratory alone. He looked distraught, like a child that had just been punished. He didn't say anything. He just walked up to the table and began to weep. His cries slowly turned into laughter. Popov raised his head to look at the camera. His eyes were now a deep yellow. Suddenly, the doctor swiped at the camera and the screen went black.

"Any idea what Col. Jackson said to him?" Harvey asked.

"I'm not sure. There are normally some security cameras in different rooms of the base, but it looks like all of those files are gone.

Whatever it was, it may have accelerated the doctor going over the edge as you can see here."

[Log12012048/Aldrin/W. Popov]

Harvey thought that the video was paused for a second. It started with Dr. Popov sitting in his chair, staring at the camera. His pale complexation and yellow eyes were almost piercing.

"I had a very unfortunate conversation with Lieutenant Colonel Scott Jackson today. It appears Dr. Chang has gone behind my back and painted me in a very unflattering light to the colonel. I don't entirely blame her for this. People are always scared of that which they do not understand. I just hope that before this is all over, I can make them understand. I don't do these things for me, oh no. I do them for her. And until they realize that, they are no better than mindless sheep. I'll make them see, make them all see. Lycaon will not be denied."

Dr. Popov smiled at the camera, showing the slightest hint of fangs, before reaching over to turn it off.

Harvey sat back in his chair and let out a long sigh.

"Is there anything after that?"

"Nothing except for a few automated logs from the security system. It looks like Dr. Popov left the base with Banks and Simmons shortly after the solar storm was done. According to the log, they were going to collect samples in the cavern. Dr. Popov returned almost half an hour later, and the system indicates that he was alone. Fifteen minutes later, Colonel Jackson's suit registered as leaving the facility. I am assuming that was Dr. Chang, because there is no indication of her leaving later on. A couple of minutes later, the system detected an anomaly in the laboratory hub. My best guess is that is when the explosion occurred. That's everything the system showed happening before you guys got here for the rescue mission."

"Fuck..." Harvey went to go rub his forehead with his left hand before remembering that it was no longer there.

"Okay, so we have no way of contacting NASA, our supplies are very limited, and we are still surrounded by seemingly indestructible werewolves. So, what's our next move?"

"As far as I can tell, we don't have one," Sanjay replied.

"No, come on, there has to be something. There's got to be something that we're overlooking here. Something that we can use against them so we can buy a little bit more time and—"

"—*and nothing, Harvey!*" Sanjay yelled. "Even if we can buy little bit of time, even if we can somehow contact NASA, we are utterly and absolutely fucked. We don't have any way to get off the moon. Our best shot is somehow getting to Collins Base and even then, we're just prolonging the inevitable. The only way that we get off the moon is if somebody comes and gets us. We can't hold out for NASA. They would have to build a new spacecraft to come grab us and you know as well as I do that the Gateway craft isn't an option right now. Even if they did come and get us, there's still the small problem of the fucking werewolves. Face it, Harvey, might as well get comfortable and accept our fate. Hell, maybe we should just find a hole to go die in. Those caverns seem big enough."

Harvey stood up suddenly.

"Whoa, whoa, whoa, what was that last part?"

"Die in a hole?"

"No! The caverns, we can use the caverns!"

"I'm not following..."

"Look, we know that these things can regenerate. The only thing that seems to work is cutting off their heads, but if we can trap them in the caverns, that'll give us enough time to plan our next move."

Sanjay stared at Harvey in confusion.

"Okay, let's say we do get them in the caverns... How are we going to trap them there?"

"By blowing them up, of course."

"And how the hell are we going to do that? You got any spare dynamite lying around?"

"No, I don't, but the fine folks of Aldrin Base might. This was a mining facility, remember? How do you think they were able to blow the lab up? They must have explosive ingredients outside the base.

It's probably in the rover garage. That's why it was built away from the base and not connected like ours is."

Sanjay stood up from his chair and started pacing, pondering Harvey's plan.

"Okay, but that doesn't solve any of our issues. How the hell are we going to get the explosives into the cavern without being mauled to death?"

"That's the easiest part. I can use the rovers."

Harvey walked over to the command console and began typing on the keyboard. It was slow, with only one hand, but he managed. The video logs disappeared and were replaced by multiple screens showing the statuses of different rovers.

"Fuck yeah! It's just as I thought. The solar storm didn't damage the rovers, at least not all of them. Hell, we even have a few inside that we could use. We can use the rovers outside to transport the explosives into the caverns. These things are built for it, it wouldn't even be that difficult to set the charges. As long as we are stealthy about it, the wolves shouldn't even notice what we are doing. We just gotta get them down there and then we can detonate the charges. After that, I can fix the communications so we can contact NASA. Worst-case scenario, we don't kill them but they are trapped under there. Best-case scenario, we're finally able to finish these things off."

"Okay, this is sounding less and less crazy, but there's just one problem. How the hell are we going to get them down there?"

"That's the only downside of this plan. We are more than likely going to have to be the bait..."

"Of course we are..."

18

The astronauts spent the next few hours putting their plan into motion. Harvey had been able to activate one of the nearby rovers to collect the explosives from the garage. The small rover then fell in with the others doing tasks around base to avoid suspicion from the wolves. These rovers were on a set timer, so their activity wasn't as suspicious. They did simple things like collect rock samples or work on the Firefly display. The wolves had been patrolling the base's perimeter, checking and rechecking it for weak points. After it was out of sight, Harvey sent the rover into the caverns. From there, it was simply a matter of having the rover distribute the explosive compound to a few strategic points within the tunnels. Each explosive was wired into the battery of a digging rover that was currently shut off. All Harvey and Sanjay had to do was turn the rover on and the electrical jolt would be enough to trigger the explosion. They just hoped that when the time came, they were far enough out of the cave.

"Okay, one more time, Harvey," Sanjay said as he checked the integrity of his EVA suit for what had to be the twelfth time.

"Alright, we enter the cave and run straight for sixty-four paces, then turn right for twenty-seven paces, then left for ten, then right again, then..."

"Left, Harvey, then we turn left!" Sanjay interrupted with a hint of annoyance in his voice. Harvey didn't take it personally, though. To say the man was stressed would be an understatement. Sanjay had come a long way from their first day of astronaut training, where he'd started out as the quiet guy that looked like he would lose a fight to a napkin. The last few days, he had survived multiple attacks, a shuttle crash, and even sawed a werewolf in two. He did this all while doing his best to take care of his crewmates. Harvey wouldn't be alive right now if it wasn't for Sanjay. Worst yet, he might even be a member of Dr. Popov's dreaded pack if it hadn't been for his impromptu surgery.

"I got it, Sanjay, don't worry! We make a left and then we run like hell out the other end. We are going to have the guidance on our wrists the entire time. Even if I forget, these things will light the way." Harvey raised what remained of his mangled hand to Sanjay, displaying the navigation screen on his wrist. "This is going to work, buddy. It has to."

"I know. I'm just... I just don't want to die up here, man. I don't want this all to be for nothing. And there's so much that could go wrong."

"I know, Sanjay. I'm just as scared as you are. Now, I don't know if this will work. Between dynamite or the rovers, there is so much room for error. Remember what the commander used to say: no plan survives first contact with the enemy. But we have a chance to get even with those sons a bitches, and I want to take full advantage of that. Regardless of what happens to us, I know one thing, and that's that these things have to die up here. I don't want them kill anyone else that might come to the moon.

Sanjay said nothing. No words were needed; now was the time for action. The two men spent the next hour checking their gear and going through the plan to the point of exhaustion.

Popov was still feeling the effects from his encounter with Commander Sanders. She had put up a valiant fight but, in the end, she had succumbed just like all of his previous prey.

The shuttle crash had burned off most of the skin from his bones. Half of his face was nothing but bone, with a few stray tendons and his retina trying to reform. His body was still healing, and he would not be able to fully regenerate until his next meal. He refused to show any weakness in front of the other, however. Banks stood just a few feet away from the doctor. Unlike Popov, who remained almost perfectly still, Captain Banks was beginning to feel the effects of failing to reach the next mutation. He had been unsuccessful in capturing his prey earlier and because of this, the captain was still weak. The only meal that he'd had was the broken Dr. Chang. Now, the captain was struggling to stand upright. He was doing his best to control his body's shaking withdrawal symptoms, but it was no use. Popov had already noticed the captain's weakened state. As far as the doctor was concerned, that was his price for failure. He had failed and was getting weaker by the minute. If he did not eat something in the next few days, his body would begin to wither away. Popov didn't care what happened to Banks. He did, however, consider the possibility that he would have to be the one to kill him if they couldn't get inside Aldrin Base. Even though Banks had not mutated further, Popov wasn't sure if he would be able to fully dispatch him in his own weakened state.

Banks sensed Popov's gaze upon him and moved to a more defensive position. Dr. Popov didn't move. He only stared at the pack member in an attempt to size him up. The captain must have sensed Dr. Popov's intentions because he had extended his claws, and the hair on his back stood on edge. Popov remained perfectly still, not wanting to give any possible advantage to the other. Before they had turned, Banks had been an accomplished soldier in the prime of his youth while Popov was anything but. Despite his brilliant mind, the doctor's best years were behind him. He was no longer the physical specimen he once prided himself in being. That all changed, however, when they were given the Gift of Lycaon. The doctor was the first to eat and as a result, he'd become the mightiest among his pack. Now that he had received the gift, the doctor wanted nothing more than to continue his feast so that he may expand his power. He allowed his claws to extend so he would be ready for Banks's attack.

To the wolves, it became clear that only one of them was going to walk away from this fight. Just as Banks began to shift his weight for an attack, the front doors of Aldrin Base began to open.

All sense and reason left them as they sprinted toward the opening door. Whether it was a malfunction or an escape attempt mattered not. They would find their prey and feed on the flesh. All while singing the praises of Artemis. The pack was just a few feet from the door when the rover emerged.

Another machine, another distraction, Popov thought. He wondered if they were dumb enough to try the same trick twice. It wouldn't matter. He would kill whatever man or machine drove the rover. He brought his large claw out and prepared to swipe. This device was clearly meant as a distraction, a distraction that would be quickly neutralized, but not by him. Popov slowed his advance and allowed Banks to take the lead. Popov noticed the sawblades as soon as Banks lunged through the air. The rover's side compartments opened to reveal four mechanical arms with a spinning blade on each. By the time Banks realized it, it was too late. Popov could hear the yelps of his pack member as the saw blade ripped his arm off. This gave the doctor a feeling of disgust. He should have killed this welp instead of Dr. Chang. At least she would've been useful.

Banks avoided the other blades and used his other arm to flip the rover. He punched and clawed at the hunk of metal until it ceased to operate, and then he started to eat the wires and screws inside the rover. Popov was disgusted with this pathetic excuse of a predator. He would have more luck killing this runt and hunting the remaining astronauts on his own. Just as he was about to do just that, he saw two shapes running toward the cave entrance off on the horizon.

It's them! Without hesitation, he barked at Banks. The captain had given up eating the rover and was now trying to reattach his severed arm, but his body was too weak to heal itself. The alpha's bark made Banks cower at first. Popov barked again and motioned toward the cave before running off on all-fours. Banks saw the two astronauts descending into the cave and hurried after the alpha.

Harvey and Sanjay ran down the surprisingly wide lunar tunnel.

"Well, it sure as shit got their attention! Here they come, Sanjay!" Harvey looked at the cave route displayed on his wrist. He was struggling to keep up with Sanjay. Harvey had suggested that Sanjay hold the detonator while he managed the bladed rover. It made sense considering Sanjay had two hands to work with as opposed to Harvey's one. There was also the morbid reality that Harvey was feeling quite weak after losing his limb. Besides IV fluids, he hadn't eaten anything in the last few days. He didn't want to risk getting caught by the werewolves and failing to detonate the explosives. This way, he figured that at least Sanjay could escape while he took revenge on the bastards that had killed his friends.

"How will we know when to start the detonation?" Sanjay asked.

Harvey looked back and almost on cue, he saw the wolves turn the first corner. Although clearly determined, the wolves were struggling to move within the tunnels. Popov's mutated form was almost too big, and he struggled to not hit his head on the ceiling. Banks was doing his best to keep up but was having difficulty maneuvering around the large monster.

"Fuck! Not yet! Just wait a bit longer," Harvey yelled. If the detonation went off now, the two men would be trapped in the caves. They needed to at least make it around the next bend if they were going to have any chance of surviving. Harvey could see the next turn up ahead.

"Sanjay, as soon as you turn that corner, you blast the shit out of this place."

Sanjay didn't argue. In fact, he didn't say anything. He only started to run faster, seemingly motivated by Harvey's command. Harvey was doing his best to keep up but was struggling. For a split-second, he almost called it quits to turn around and face the beasts head-on. To die like a man. That thought quickly disappeared when he thought about how his friends had died. The bravest, toughest people he had ever met, and each one of them died screaming in agony. Sanjay turned the corner, and Harvey began to feel the ground tremble beneath him.

Fuck yeah, he did it! Harvey thought. If his adrenaline hadn't spiked before, it did now. He turned the corner and saw only light protruding from the exit. As he ran toward his salvation, he looked back to see the walls of the cave crashing down. The werewolves were being peppered with lunar rock. Popov had that same sick look of determination on his face as he continued to run toward Harvey. He reached toward him, trying to pull him back into the dark abyss with them. Harvey turned back toward the light only to see another hand extended toward him. Harvey reached for Sanjay as far as he could, and he almost let out a sigh of relief when Sanjay wrapped his fingers around his wrist. The world went silent as Sanjay pulled Harvey from the cave so hard that he flew through the air. The two men hit the lunar surface as the cave behind them crumbled in on itself, sending dust and debris flying.

Harvey only saw the dust floating through the air. He started to stand, using his left arm to push himself up but forgetting again about his missing hand. Luckily, Sanjay was there to break his fall. Sanjay grabbed Harvey by the shoulder and helped him to his feet. The two men said nothing for a while. They only looked at the cave as they waited for the dust to settle. After a few seconds, the visibility cleared up enough to show that the cave's exit had been completely destroyed. The amount of rubble and stone protruding from the once wide opening made it look like the cave had never even existed. Harvey heard Sanjay begin to laugh. It was a loud and infectious laugh and before Harvey knew it, he was laughing as well. He could feel the tears begin to well up in his eyes and did his best to suppress them, but it was no good. They had been through so much, lost so much, and just like that, it was finally over. The two men continued laughing for a while longer before Sanjay finally broke the celebration with a question.

"So... What do we do now?"

Harvey answered in between laughter. "Honestly? I didn't think that we would get this far. I guess we can see about getting the comms back and trying to rendezvous with Gateway. If that doesn't work, then maybe we can use the railgun to launch ourselves into space."

Harvey pointed at the horizon to railgun system that was used to fire valuable resources and equipment back to Earth. He knew it would be a suicidal attempt but couldn't help himself from making a joke.

"Solid plan. Let's go check the comms first, just to be on the safe si—"

Harvey felt a powerful force knock him off his feet. The world spun for a few seconds while his body tumbled along the hard surface. He tried to get up but once again forgot about it his missing hand. He began to steady himself and looked toward Sanjay to ask what happened. Harvey saw Sanjay standing a few feet in front of him, surrounded by lunar dust.

"Sanjay! What was tha—"

Sanjay began to float toward Harvey, his body mostly hidden by the dust. It wasn't until he got a bit closer that Harvey's worst fears were realized. Popov's deformed face stared at Harvey, his yellow eye piercing into him. The wolf had his jaws wrapped around Sanjay's neck. His claws dug into the man's shoulders.

"Harvey..." Sanjay rasped, his throat filling with blood. "Run..."

19

Harvey screamed at Popov. All the anger and emotion that had been building up these last few days had finally broken free. Harvey sprinted as fast as he could toward Sanjay and the werewolf. There was no plan, only instinct. Harvey was sick and tired of being prey to these monsters. It didn't take long for him to close the gap. He clenched his fist as he came up to Popov and poor Sanjay. Harvey was ready to throw a haymaker. He was going to knock out this monster with one punch—at least that was how he felt until Popov swung his giant skeletal claw at Harvey's torso.

The astronaut lost all feeling in that moment as he flew almost a hundred feet through the air. The numbness disappeared as soon as he slammed into lunar surface. The air escaped his lungs, his ribs cracked, and his shoulder dislocated on impact. The werewolf looked like he was swatting at Harvey the way somebody would swat at a fly. He had thrown every ounce of rage and strength he had left at the monster, and it was little more than an annoyance.

That was fucking dumb, he thought. Despite his immediate injuries, Harvey tried his best to stand up. His eyes immediately went back to Sanjay. Dr. Popov was ravaging the man's lifeless body. It was a bloodlust-filled feeding frenzy. Like so many before him, Sanjay's last moments of horror were permanently frozen on his face—a side effect of his suit being ripped open. Popov grinned as he ripped into what used to be a human being. Harvey found himself once more thankful for the vacuum of space so he didn't have to listen to the crunching of Sanjay's limbs as the wolf bent and twisted them to his sick desires. Suddenly, Popov's gaze went from Sanjay to Harvey. This snapped Harvey out of whatever daze he had previously been in, and the astronaut began to limp away. Every step Harvey took caused his body to scream in agony. His labored breathes made him pretty sure that he had broken at least one rib. His bad arm had been dislocated, and now his left leg was going numb. He wanted to run, but his body wouldn't let him. He wanted to hide, but there was nowhere left to go. He needed help, but there was no one left to help. Harvey was good and well fucked.

Popov couldn't help but smile as he watched his next victim hobble away. These last two astronauts had fought well. They were more than worthy of the Gift of Lycaon, but unfortunately for them, Popov needed to eat if he had any hope of surviving. He felt the muscles of his face contract once more as his flesh began to heal the skeletal side of his body. Within seconds, his vision was returned to perfection as his left eye grew back. He looked down at his once-deformed arm. What had previously been nothing more than bone and burnt flesh had now been returned to its previous glory. The doctor lifted his head toward the emptiness of space and began to howl. It was a howl that only he and his goddess could hear. He would slaughter the injured rabbit and then he would find the last survivor and use him as the final sacrifice. First, though, he was going to enjoy himself. Popov went down on all-fours and took off into a sprint.

Harvey was trying to control himself, trying to not let the fear rule him. He needed a plan, needed to find somewhere to escape this monster. No matter what thought he put into the void of his mind, the only thing he got back was: *You're fucked, kid!*

The hit came from his side. He didn't have to guess what caused it. Harvey was knocked across ground, seemingly hitting every single rock formation in the process before he slid to a slow stop.

When did the Moon get so smooth?

Harvey quickly realized where he was. Popov had knocked him right on to Aldrin Base's solar panels—the very same panels designed to convert solar energy into powerful microwaves and then revolutionize clean energy on Earth...once scientists worked out a few kinks.

"Firefly!" he whispered. The voices in Harvey's head finally quieted as a plan started to form. He looked at the wrist display on his bad arm and began to type.

"Please, please, please, please, please..." He prayed out loud to any god, demon, or fictional character that was listening. Harvey used his wrist computer to access Aldrin Base's functions. When Sanjay reactivated the base's security systems, he had turned on all of the base's other features, such as rovers, life support, and with any luck, the Firefly display. Harvey looked up at Popov, who was stalking toward him. The wolf still had that menacing grin on his face. He was clearly amused with himself as he kept moving his claws. It was almost like he was warming them up. Harvey rapidly clicked through Aldrin's systems until he found what he was looking for. He clicked on the ACTIVATE FIREFLY PANEL SYSTEM button on the display, followed by the activate command. His screen then read FIREFLY PANEL SEQUENCE INITIATED. PANELS WILL FIRE IN 60 SECONDS, and it began to count down.

"Yes!" he shouted. The panels must have been full of energy from the solar storm that had terrorized everyone for the last few weeks.

Now all I have to do is wait.

Harvey felt another powerful blow to his body, knocking him off his feet. If his ribs weren't broken before, they were now. He came crashing down on the panels with such force that they cracked from his impact. Harvey opened his eyes to see Popov jumping into the air, ready to inflict a massive stomp to his body. Before, Harvey had been content with keeping the doctor busy long enough for the panels to discharge, killing him and Dr. Popov in the process. Something about seeing the werewolf jumping through the air with a sick look of pleasure on his face changed Harvey's mind. He wanted to live. He wanted to stick it to this fucking demon and survive long enough to watch him burn to a crisp. He wanted to avenge his friends and write a tell-all book on how he saved the day and Greg was an asshole. He wanted to do all those things, and so, he decided that he was going to fight. Not the way that Mike or the commander had fought, though. His injuries were too great and even on his best day, he knew he'd be no match for the good doctor. No, he needed to play to his strengths if he was going to have any chance of surviving.

Harvey rolled out of the way as Popov came crashing down on the panels, shattering them in the process. Harvey raced to his feet, trying to run as fast as he could. He wasn't looking at the horizon, though. Instead, his gaze was fixated on his wrist's display screen. He needed to enter this next command perfectly if he was going to have any chance.

He felt a large hand grab the back of his suit and was flung once more through the air. He landed on the panels again but was able to keep his posture somewhat. His mind was fixated on the task at hand. He would worry about his injuries later.

He frantically pressed commands into his wrist. Just one wrong instruction and he was as good as dead.

He entered the final command and hit enter.

Harvey let out a sigh of relief that quickly disappeared when a huge shadow appeared over him. The astronaut looked up to see the same sick, bloody smile that had plagued him these last few days. The same smile that had been the last thing Mike, Sanjay, and Sanders saw as they were ripped apart. Looking at the wolf up close now, Harvey saw no sign of regret on his face. He was savoring this moment, just as he had with all his other kills. He enjoyed playing with his food. He enjoyed the pain, the fear, the turmoil... He enjoyed it all. Still, something about the way the doctor was standing told Harvey that this was it. This would be where he finished it. As Popov raised his massive arm, his sick smile never wavered. The arm was brought down with thunderous strength that would have sliced through his prey with ease. Harvey felt the bones in his hand break. His body was screaming louder and louder at him but somehow, he had caught the monster's strike. Despite his broken bones, Harvey did his best to hold on to the wolf's arm, shaking as he did.

Popov looked at Harvey more in annoyance then actual disbelief.

This insolent creature had evaded him at every turn. Now, even when faced with no options, he was still fighting. Normally, the doctor would admire such fortitude, but not right now. Right now, the animal was angry. Angry at this little runt, this rabbit, for trying to deny him his kill. He was out of options and out of time. The fact that he was not laying down and accepting his fate was an insult to Popov and Artemis.

Breaking free of Harvey's grasp, Popov brought his massive claw around Harvey's good arm. He grabbed the man's limp arm and lifted him so they were now face-to-face. Harvey felt pain radiating through his body as the wolf methodically pulled his good arm from his socket. He now hung in the monster's grasp, unable to fight back. He could feel his upper body going numb from the pain. He screamed in agony as the werewolf stared in delight. Popov began to open his mouth, red slobber dripping, already salivating his next meal. Harvey could only scream and look on in horror. He wanted to kick, to fight somehow, but the pain was too much. His body would longer respond to his commands.

The wolf's mouth inched closer to Harvey, his jaw now fully extended. He was about to close his serrated teeth on his prey when something crashed into him from the side, sending him off balance. Before Popov could see what hit him, he felt another object bang into his other side. The second hit caused him to unceremoniously drop Harvey. Popov looked down in anger, expecting to find more prey only to see two large mining rovers circling him. Unlike the bladed rover from earlier, these two each possessed powerful robotic arms that were used to move large deposits of lunar rock. He clawed at the approaching rover, knocking it back a few feet. He then looked over to see Harvey, who was doing his best to crawl away. Harvey got to his feet as quickly as he could and looked down at his wrist.

FIREFLY DISPLAY WILL FIRE IN 11 SECONDS.

The clock was ticking, and he had to get off these solar panels if he hoped to avoid being barbequed. He could see the edge of the panels just a few feet away. He'd almost used these two rovers earlier to help distract the werewolves. Like the bladed rover from earlier, these two were designed to assist with the mining efforts. After the caves were blasted with explosives, these rovers were programed to travel through the tunnels and clear out any large debris. The operator just needed to specify the location for the rovers to go and how large the object was. You could even program them to work together to move very large debris, which Popov was finding out. On a football field-sized area, Popov was the biggest thing the rovers could see.

FIREFLY DISPLAY WILL FIRE IN 8 SECONDS.

Dr. Popov went into a feral rage as he charged after Harvey, only to have his foot caught by the second rover, sending him to his knees. The wolf kicked at the rover with his free foot, which was quickly latched onto by the other rover.

FIREFLY DISPLAY WILL FIRE IN 5 SECONDS.

Popov could feel the ground beneath him starting to warm up. Whatever shred of his former self still lied within began to panic. He didn't know why, but he knew that he had to get off this unnatural ground as soon as possible. He looked toward his limping prey and growled.

FIREFLY DISPLAY WILL FIRE IN 3 SECONDS.

He refused to be bested by such a weak creature. He thrashed violently, knocking one rover to its side. He was now able to wrap his claws around the other. He slashed into the mechanical nuisance until all signs of life left it.

FIREFLY DISPLAY WILL FIRE IN 2 SECONDS.

As soon as Harvey stepped off the solar panels, he turned to see that Popov had gotten to his feet. He had dispatched one rover and managed to shake off the other.

FIREFLY DISPLAY WILL FIRE IN 1 SECOND.

The wolf ran with every ounce of speed his body would allow. Within an instant, he had closed the forty-foot gap between him and his prey. As he slashed wildly at Harvey, a bright light appeared beneath him. For the first time since receiving the Gift of Lycaon, Dr. Popov experienced fear.

FIREFLY DISPLAY INITIATED.

The panels erupted with intense, white heat. The last thing Harvey saw was a large claw swinging toward his face before the light nearly blinded him. Popov let out an agonized scream as his fur and skin disappeared, revealing a grotesque skeleton. Within seconds, that too was melted away, leaving no remains except for the large claw that had tried to latch onto Harvey before the blast. Now the claw rested on the ground, forever frozen in its last attempt at slaughter. Harvey stared at the claw for a few seconds, waiting for it to show any signs of life. When it didn't, he finally let out a sigh of relief. Suddenly, it became difficult for him to stand. With his adrenaline wearing off, he was quickly becoming all too aware of the many injuries he had suffered. Both of his shoulders were dislocated, his ribs were broken, he couldn't feel his left leg at all, and was that blood he saw? Was it his?

Harvey sat on the lunar surface. He looked at his wrist display and checked his air supply. He was running low.

That would explain why it's getting so hard to breathe...

He knew that he should get to Aldrin Base as fast as possible, that its life support system was his only chance, but no matter how much he wanted to, he just couldn't seem to get back up. Instead, he just sat on the cold lunar surface. He was too tired to move, and he could feel his breathing growing shallow. Harvey looked up into the abyss of space and marveled at its beauty.

As far as last sights go, this one isn't too shabby.

As his vision faded, Harvey imagined that he was back on Earth, with Jessica and the rest of the team running through another exercise. It was a beautiful day, and Harvey even thought he felt a cool breeze on his face. Jessica grabbed his hand and gave it a squeeze.

"It's okay, Harvey! You're going to be okay! We're here!"

20

Dr. Holstrom struggled to keep control of the rover as it came upon the Collins Communication Array. He had many strengths as an accomplished scientist but operating the rover was not among them. To say that these last few days were difficult would be an understatement. The wolf chased after him for almost a full day. Dr. Holstrom led him around the lunar surface in hopes that he would tire himself out. He didn't want to risk the wolf following him all the way to Collins. He was eventually able to get far enough away from the wolf that he could make his way to Collins without worrying about being caught. The only problem was that the LTV had almost completely run out of usable air tanks. There was no way that his air supply would last long enough for him to make it to Collins.

With little other options, Dr. Holstrom's only chance was to return to Armstrong Base and salvage whatever air and resources he could. He parked far enough from Armstrong that he could observe it from a safe distance. He wanted to be absolutely sure that nothing was waiting for him there. After no movement for a few hours, he decided that it was safe to drive into the base's perimeter. He made his way towards the Armstrong supply crates and stocked up on as many air cannisters that the LTV could handle. It was the riskiest thing that he had ever done, but he managed to make it out alive.

The next hardship Dr. Holstrom faced was actually finding Collins. What should have been the easiest part of his salvation proved to be the most difficult. For almost forty-eight hours, Dr. Holstrom drove around the lunar surface looking for the array. The LTV's navigation hadn't worked since the shuttle crash, forcing him to use a map. The map must have been out of date though, because try as he might, he just kept getting lost. On two occasions, he somehow circled back to the Armstrong area, only to realize his mistake. After forty-eight hours of hopelessly driving around, the exhausted Dr. Holstrom finally found the Collins Communication Array. It was the most beautiful sight he had ever seen, or at least it was, until he crashed.

He came over the hill and immediately swerved to avoid a large crevice in front of the base. Despite his best efforts, the front tire of the LTV still got caught in the hole. The sudden stop almost launched Dr. Holstrom out of his seat.

"Fuck!" He slammed his fist against the steering wheel. "Can no one make a piece of machinery that works properly?"

Holstrom looked around the horizon. After his last encounter with the wolf, he would not be taking any chances. To his relief, he saw no signs of life around him. The doctor unhooked himself and walked to the front of the vehicle to assess for damage. He believed that it was still drivable but getting it out of the crevice would prove difficult, even in lunar gravity. Perhaps if some of his crew was still around, he would be able to.

Maybe if I didn't leave Jessica behind...

No! No! Stop thinking like that. Jessica was as good as dead. There was no way that she would've made it to the rover before the creature caught up to her. If I had waited, then there would've been zero survivors in this mission. I lived because I did what was necessary. It's what made me a good leader. If only the buffoons at NASA would've realized that, then maybe the crew would still be alive. Unfortunately for them, they chose to side with the unpredictable Commander Sanders. Now they are reaping the consequences.

Holstrom made his way to the front door and opened the security panel. Unlike the other bases, the Collins Communication Array did not have a crew constantly stationed there. When not occupied, the base served as an emergency shelter should anything happen to the other two bases. Members from both crews received the appropriate security codes so they could enter the base during such emergencies.

He entered the code into the keypad and the front doors started to open. The doctor entered the airlock and waited for the all-clear. The airlock played a familiar chime, indicating that the base's life-support system was working. Dr. Holstrom removed his helmet and for the first time in what felt like forever, he breathed fresh air. The exhaustion hit Dr. Holstrom all at once. He wanted nothing more right now then to pass out in a comfy bed. He knew that he had before he could do that though, that he needed to radio for help.

Lights turned on throughout the base, illuminating its neat, white interior. The doctor made his way to the command center so he could try and get a hold of someone at NASA. It had been a long journey and soon it would be over. He sat in front of the desk and began entering commands into the computer. The system was working well enough, except for the communications. Every time he tried to send a message to NASA or Gateway, it failed to go through. After multiple attempts, Holstrom started to slam his fists on the console.

"How in the flying fuck does a communications array not have any communications?"

Then he remembered the small communications station he'd walked past on his way in, and that was when it all started to make sense.

Of course, the comms were damaged during the solar storm. They need to be rebooted. I walked right past the comm station outside and didn't think anything of it. Come on, Greg, you're better than this!

Holstrom started to put his gear back on. He didn't really know how to repair the communications array, but he figured if Harvey could do it then he should be able to figure it out. He waited for the room to depressurize once more before opening the front door back to the surface. He stepped outside cautiously, looking for anything dangerous or out of the ordinary. After deciding that the coast was clear, he sprinted toward the display, not wanting to dillydally in the slightest. *It's okay! I just need a few seconds to look over the display.*

Everything seemed to be in working order, but he just couldn't figure out what was causing the issue. After studying the equipment some more, he realized the problem.

"Surely it can't be that easy?"

He flipped the switch toward the center of the array into the "on" position. To his delight, the array started to power up. The satellite fields to his right began to shift, indicating that they were searching for a signal.

Seriously? That's it? An on switch. Why did we have to suffer the likes of that imbecile if any one of us could've done his job to begin with.

Holstrom made his way back to base, laughing at himself as he went. He was practically a one-man crew, just as he always thought. Now all he had to do was get in contact with NASA and wait for the rescue mission. Hopefully, he wouldn't have to wait too long. Sure the base was full of supplies, but the sooner he got off the moon, the better. There would be questions of course and he would be more than happy to give the answers. He would tell them how the commander completely disregarded his suggestions—suggestions that would've undoubtedly saved the crew. He would tell them how they wasted valuable resources on a half-assed plan to destroy the monsters. Then he would tell them his brave account of how he desperately tried to save the lives of his remaining crewmates, only for the wolves to get there first. After the investigation concluded, no doubt labeling Dr. Holstrom a hero, he looked forward to his new life. He would dine with senators, entertainers, and other bigwigs. Everyone would be lined up to sing the praises of the great Dr. Holstrom, the lone survivor of Artemis. Just like everything else in life, Dr. Gregory Holstrom was going to come out of this on top

Dr. Holstrom walked past the crevice that he had crashed the LTV into, only to realize that the vehicle was much more damaged than he previously realized. The back wheels had almost been slashed through entirely. It was surely a miracle that he had been able to drive it for as long as he did. He made his way around to the front of the rover and saw that the front tires had also been slashed. That was when the doctor came to a dreadful conclusion.

Something had attacked the rover since he'd arrived here. He looked around but saw nothing. He sprinted toward the airlock and entered the code. As he waited for the door to open, he looked back at his surroundings. He saw no sign of any life anywhere. Then he looked down at the lunar surface. He saw his tracks leading from the front door of the base to the communications array, but he also noticed something else. There was a second pair of tracks leading from the front of the base toward the rover. These tracks were thin, almost bird-like. That was when Dr. Gregory Holstrom, lone survivor, came to a second conclusion.

Whatever attacked the rover came from inside the base...

Dr. Holstrom turned as the airlock doors opened. Standing in front of him was a large monstrosity covered in fur and wearing shreds of what appeared to be a burnt blue jumpsuit. Holstrom turned to run away, but it was too late. The wolf grabbed him by the shoulder, digging his claws in. The man let out a scream as he was thrown into the airlock. His back slammed into the doors so hard that they almost crashed open. The doctor slid across the hallway, his shoulder burning in pain.

The radio! I have to get to the radio!

Dr. Holstrom crawled to the console and started to input commands. Tears began to flow as he grabbed the microphone and began to speak.

"Mayday! Mayday! Mayday! Mayday! NASA, this is a Dr. Gregory Holstrom. I'm at the Collins Communication—"

Holstrom's voice was cut off by a loud growl from behind him. He turned to see the werewolf standing over him once more. It stretched out its hand and dug its claws into the man's shoulder wound. Dr. Holstrom screamed in agony as the monster lifted him into the air. The pain was so intense that the doctor lost control of his bladder onto the pristine white floor. If the wolf cared, he didn't show it as he brought his grinning jaw toward the man's face. The last sound that Gregory Holstrom would ever hear would be his uncontrollable wails for help as Lt. Colonel Jackson ripped him apart.

21

Harvey awoke to the familiar noise of an EKG machine. He was groggy at first, but a familiar voice pulled him out of it.

"It's okay, Harvey. You're safe now," Jessica said.

"Jessica! You're... You're alive!" said an exhausted Harvey. He wiped at his eyes. His vision still blurry.

"No... It's Amelia, Amelia Ortiz. You're on Gateway, Harvey. You were the only one that we found alive."

Harvey blinked a few times, allowing his vision to adjust. He was lying in the infirmary of Gateway Space Station. Sitting next to him was Captain Amelia Ortiz, Gateway's second-in-command.

"I'm...the only one?" Harvey felt a pit open in his stomach, and he began to cry. Amelia reached over to grab his hand to console him. *Of course I'm the only one,* he thought. The memories of his friends' death flooding back to him.

"Colonel," Amelia called. Within seconds, the door to the infirmary opened and in walked Lieutenant Colonel Phil Hannon.

"Harvey, I'm glad you're awake. You've been through a hell of an ordeal, son. For what it's worth, I'm sorry."

Harvey did his best to collect himself. He had questions that couldn't wait. He wiped the tears from his eyes and began to speak.

"How...how did you rescue me? We couldn't get the communications to work. How did you even know where to find me?"

"We did our best to track you on satellite. When the shuttle crashed, it threw everything into a tailspin. We had to make an emergency maneuver just to avoid the damn thing ourselves. It wasn't until you fired off that solar panel display that we were able to pinpoint your location."

"How did you get to me, though?"

"We used the second shuttle to come grab you."

"I thought that thing was only designed for Earth reentry. NASA approved you using it for that?"

"No... Harvey, I'm not going to lie. We broke a lot of protocols by rescuing you the way we did. I know it might seem like too little too late, but the whole team did whatever we could. I will more than likely be facing some sort of non-judicial punishment when we get back to Earth. Hopefully the fact that the rescue mission was a success will buy me some points."

Harvey did his best to control his emotions. He knew that the Gateway crew had risked a lot just to save him. He knew that they wished they could've done more. None of that changed the fact that he still felt pain in his stomach—pain from the guilt that he had lived and everyone else had died.

"Thank you," was all Harvey could manage at the moment.

"Don't thank me yet. NASA and everyone else are going to have a whole shit ton of questions for you—myself included. Right now, though, you need to rest. I've instructed Amelia to take care of you. Whenever you're ready to talk, you let me know. Until then, we are here for you."

"Thank you, sir. I appreciate it. I really do. Tell me, do you know what happened to Dr. Holstrom?"

"Not yet. We saw from the satellite images that one of the crew got away in a rover. We weren't sure who it was. Last we heard from NASA, it looked like it was heading towards Collins."

"He left her... He could've saved her but instead he left her. If he's still alive, I wanna be there when he's questioned."

"We'll cross that bridge when we come to it, Harvey. Right now, I just want you to—"

A panicked crew member barged into the infirmary.

"Colonel, we need you at the command center. It's..."

The man glanced at Harvey before looking back at Colonel Hannon.

"We are getting a message from the Collins Communication Array."

The colonel walked to the door.

"Harvey, get some rest. I'll brief you later," he said before he and the crew member left the infirmary.

Harvey wanted to follow the colonel. He wanted to be the first voice that Greg heard so that he knew full well that he couldn't spew any of his typical bullshit and try and paint himself as a hero. He started to sit up before he caught a glimpse of the Moon outside the infirmary window. Suddenly, everything was so pointless. There was no point in interrogating Greg right now.

I never realized just how beautiful the Moon is.

Harvey stared out his window and took it all in. These last few days had forever changed him. He'd faced literal monsters and lived to tell about it.

It's so full, so beautiful.

He had lost his friends along the way, but they would always be remembered. He would make sure of that. He would make sure that everyone knew about the heroic deeds of Armstrong crew.

I am so hungry, and the moon is so beautiful.

"Harvey..."

And when he finally got his hands on that traitor Greg, he would make sure that everyone on Earth knew about his cowardice.

"Harvey..."

When he is done embarrassing Greg, he would beat him to a bloody pulp before tearing him limb from limb.

Then taste his blood as we rip his insides out...

"Harvey!" Amelia shouted.

Harvey turned his head toward her in surprise.

"What?"

"Are you okay? You looked like you were somewhere else for a second."

"Oh, I'm fine," Harvey answered.

He turned back to stare out his window at the lush lunar surface.

"I'm just hungry..."

If you enjoyed Lycaon then be sure to check out Wes Parker's other book

Look for the Kaiju Survival Guide on Amazon

Check out www.teepublic.com/user/mechawes for some sweet merch.

ACKNOWLEDGMENTS

The cover for Lycaon was done by the amazing José Lucas. José is always great to work with and I can't wait to work on more books with him in the future. If you would like to contact him for your next project design, you can do so at www.twitter.com/Kid_Mindfreak

The Map was created by the wonderful Niklas Wisedt. Niklas is a fellow Old School Tabletop RPG fan. Odds are that you have probably seen some of his incredible work online already and didn't even know it. If you would like to work with him on any of your future products, please reach him at www.wistedt.net

ABOUT THE AUTHOR

Wes Parker is from Armada, MI. From the moment he could talk, Wes was telling stories. Whether it was to his mother, his friends, or the family dog, Wes just liked to tell stories. Today Wes spends his time writing these stories and adventuring with his beautiful wife Tiffany. Together they have one bossy cat and two giant Labradors, who haven't quite realized they aren't lap dogs.

 twitter.com/MechaWes

instagram.com/MechaWes

www.ingramcontent.com/pod-product-compliance
Lightning Source LLC
Chambersburg PA
CBHW050742230626
47052CB00004BA/1034